THE PELICAN SHAKESPEARE
GENERAL EDITORS

STEPHEN ORGEL
A. R. BRAUNMULLER

Measure for Measure

An eighteenth-century Isabella: Mary Anne Yates
(1728–1787) at Drury Lane in the 1760s. Coached by
Garrick, she was praised for her severe dignity in the role. She
was considered the greatest tragic actress between the death of
Mrs. Cibber and the rise of Mrs. Siddons.

William Shakespeare

———

Measure for Measure

EDITED BY JONATHAN CREWE

PENGUIN BOOKS

PENGUIN BOOKS

Published by the Penguin Group Penguin Putnam Inc.,
375 Hudson Street, New York, New York 10014, U.S.A.
Penguin Books Ltd, 27 Wrights Lane, London W8 5TZ, England
Penguin Books Australia Ltd, Ringwood, Victoria, Australia
Penguin Books Canada Ltd, 10 Alcorn Avenue, Toronto, Ontario, Canada M4V 3B2
Penguin Books (N.Z.) Ltd, 182–190 Wairau Road, Auckland 10, New Zealand

Penguin Books Ltd, Registered Offices: Harmondsworth, Middlesex, England

Measure for Measure edited by R. C. Bald published in the
United States of America by Penguin Books 1956
Revised edition published 1970
This new edition edited by Jonathan Crewe published 2000

5   7   9   10   8   6   4

LIBRARY OF CONGRESS CATALOGING IN PUBLICATION DATA
Shakespeare, William, 1564–1616.
Measure for measure / William Shakespeare; edited by Jonathan Crewe.
p.   cm.—(The Pelican Shakespeare)
Includes bibliographical references.
ISBN 0 14 07.1479 0
1. Chastity—Drama.   2. Brothers and sisters—Drama.
3. Vienna (Austria)—Drama.   I. Crewe, Jonathan V.   II. Title.   III. Series.
PR2824.A2 C74   2000
822.3'3—dc21   00–033661

Printed in the United States of America
Set in Adobe Garamond
Designed by Virginia Norey

Contents

Publisher's Note

IT IS ALMOST half a century since the first volumes of the Pelican Shakespeare appeared under the general editorship of Alfred Harbage. The fact that a new edition, rather than simply a revision, has been undertaken reflects the profound changes textual and critical studies of Shakespeare have undergone in the past twenty years. For the new Pelican series, the texts of the plays and poems have been thoroughly revised in accordance with recent scholarship, and in some cases have been entirely reedited. New introductions and notes have been provided in all the volumes. But the new Shakespeare is also designed as a successor to the original series; the previous editions have been taken into account, and the advice of the previous editors has been solicited where it was feasible to do so.

Certain textual features of the new Pelican Shakespeare should be particularly noted. All lines are numbered that contain a word, phrase, or allusion explained in the glossarial notes. In addition, for convenience, every tenth line is also numbered, in italics when no annotation is indicated. The intrusive and often inaccurate place headings inserted by early editors are omitted (as is becoming standard practice), but for the convenience of those who miss them, an indication of locale now appears as the first item in the annotation of each scene.

In the interest of both elegance and utility, each speech prefix is set in a separate line when the speaker's lines are in verse, except when those words form the second half of a verse line. Thus the verse form of the speech is kept visually intact. What is printed as verse and what is printed as prose has, in general, the authority of the original texts. Departures from the original texts in this regard have only the authority of editorial tradition and the judgment of the Pelican editors; and, in a few instances, are admittedly arbitrary.

The Theatrical World

Economic realities determined the theatrical world in which Shakespeare's plays were written, performed, and received. For centuries in England, the primary theatrical tradition was nonprofessional. Craft guilds (or "mysteries") provided religious drama – mystery plays – as part of the celebration of religious and civic festivals, and schools and universities staged classical and neoclassical drama in both Latin and English as part of their curricula. In these forms, drama was established and socially acceptable. Professional theater, in contrast, existed on the margins of society. The acting companies were itinerant; playhouses could be any available space – the great halls of the aristocracy, town squares, civic halls, inn yards, fair booths, or open fields – and income was sporadic, dependent on the passing of the hat or on the bounty of local patrons. The actors, moreover, were considered little better than vagabonds, constantly in danger of arrest or expulsion.

In the late 1560s and 1570s, however, English professional theater began to gain respectability. Wealthy aristocrats fond of drama – the Lord Admiral, for example, or the Lord Chamberlain – took acting companies under their protection so that the players technically became members of their households and were no longer subject to arrest as homeless or masterless men. Permanent theaters were first built at this time as well, allowing the companies to control and charge for entry to their performances.

Shakespeare's livelihood, and the stunning artistic explosion in which he participated, depended on pragmatic and architectural effort. Professional theater requires ways to restrict access to its offerings; if it does not, and admission fees cannot be charged, the actors do not get paid, the costumes go to a pawnbroker, and there is no such thing as a professional, ongoing theatrical tradition. The answer to that economic need arrived in the late 1560s and 1570s with the creation of the so-called public or amphitheater playhouse. Recent discoveries indicate that the precursor of the Globe playhouse in London (where Shakespeare's mature plays were presented) and the Rose theater (which presented Christopher Marlowe's plays and some of Shakespeare's earliest ones) was the Red Lion theater of 1567. Archaeological studies of the foundations of the Rose and Globe theaters have revealed that the open-air theater of the 1590s and later was probably a polygonal building with fourteen to twenty or twenty-four sides, multistoried, from 75 to 100 feet in diameter, with a raised, partly covered "thrust" stage that projected into a group of standing patrons, or "groundlings," and a covered gallery, seating up to 2,500 or more (very crowded) spectators.

These theaters might have been about half full on any given day, though the audiences were larger on holidays or when a play was advertised, as old and new were, through printed playbills posted around London. The metropolitan area's late-Tudor, early-Stuart population (circa 1590-1620) has been estimated at about 150,000 to 250,000. It has been supposed that in the mid-1590s there were about 15,000 spectators per week at the public theaters; thus, as many as 10 percent of the local population went to the theater regularly. Consequently, the theaters' repertories – the plays available for this experienced and frequent audience – had to change often: in the month between September 15 and October 15, 1595, for instance, the Lord Admiral's Men performed twenty-eight times in eighteen different plays.

Since natural light illuminated the amphitheaters' stages, performances began between noon and two o'clock and ran without a break for two or three hours. They often concluded with a jig, a fencing display, or some other nondramatic exhibition. Weather conditions determined the season for the amphitheaters: plays were performed every day (including Sundays, sometimes, to clerical dismay) except during Lent – the forty days before Easter – or periods of plague, or sometimes during the summer months when law courts were not in session and the most affluent members of the audience were not in London.

To a modern theatergoer, an amphitheater stage like that of the Rose or Globe would appear an unfamiliar mixture of plainness and elaborate decoration. Much of the structure was carved or painted, sometimes to imitate marble; elsewhere, as under the canopy projecting over the stage, to represent the stars and the zodiac. Appropriate painted canvas pictures (of Jerusalem, for example, if the play was set in that city) were apparently hung on the wall behind the acting area, and tragedies were accompanied by black hangings, presumably something like crepe festoons or bunting. Although these theaters did not employ what we would call scenery, early modern spectators saw numerous large props, such as the "bar" at which a prisoner stood during a trial, the "mossy bank" where lovers reclined, an arbor for amorous conversation, a chariot, gallows, tables, trees, beds, thrones, writing desks, and so forth. Audiences might learn a scene's location from a sign (reading "Athens," for example) carried across the stage (as in Bertolt Brecht's twentieth-century productions). Equally captivating (and equally irritating to the theater's enemies) were the rich costumes and personal props the actors used: the most valuable items in the surviving theatrical inventories are the swords, gowns, robes, crowns, and other items worn or carried by the performers.

Magic appealed to Shakespeare's audiences as much as it does to us today, and the theater exploited many deceptive and spectacular devices. A winch in the loft above the stage, called "the heavens," could lower and raise actors playing gods, goddesses, and other supernatural figures to and from the main acting area, just as one or more trap-doors permitted entrances and exits to and from the area, called "hell," beneath the stage. Actors wore elementary makeup such as wigs, false beards, and face paint, and they employed pig's bladders filled with animal blood to make wounds seem more real. They had rudimentary but effective ways of pretending to behead or hang a person. Supernumeraries (stagehands or actors not needed in a particular scene) could make thunder sounds (by shaking a metal sheet or rolling an iron ball down a chute) and show lightning (by blowing inflammable resin through tubes into a flame). Elaborate fireworks enhanced the effects of dragons flying through the air or imitated such celestial phenomena as comets, shooting stars, and multi-ple suns. Horses' hoofbeats, bells (located perhaps in the tower above the stage), trumpets and drums, clocks, can-non shots and gunshots, and the like were common sound effects. And the music of viols, cornets, oboes, and recorders was a regular feature of theatrical performances.

For two relatively brief spans, from the late 1570s to 1590 and from 1599 to 1614, the amphitheaters com-peted with the so-called private, or indoor, theaters, which originated as, or later represented themselves as, educational institutions training boys as singers for church services and court performances. These indoor theaters had two features that were distinct from the am-phitheaters': their personnel and their playing spaces. The amphitheaters' adult companies included both adult men, who played the male roles, and boys, who played the female roles; the private, or indoor, theater companies, on the other hand, were entirely composed of boys aged about 8 to 16, who were, or could pretend to be, can-didates for singers in a church or a royal boys' choir. (Until 1660, professional theatrical companies included no women.) The playing space would appear much more familiar to modern audiences than the long-vanished amphitheaters; the later indoor theaters were, in fact, the ancestors of the typical modern theater. They were enclosed spaces, usually rectangular, with the stage filling one end of the rectangle and the audience arrayed in seats or benches across (and sometimes lining) the building's longer axis. These spaces staged plays less frequently than the public theaters (perhaps only once a week) and held far fewer spectators than the amphitheaters: about 200 to 600, as opposed to 2,500 or more. Fewer patrons mean a smaller gross income, unless each pays more. Not surprisingly, then, private theaters charged higher prices than the amphitheaters, probably sixpence, as opposed to a penny for the cheapest entry.

Protected from the weather, the indoor theaters presented plays later in the day than the amphitheaters, and used artificial illumination – candles in sconces or candelabra. But candles melt, and need replacing, snuffing, and trimming, and these practical requirements may have been part of the reason the indoor theaters introduced breaks in the performance, the intermission so dear to the heart of theatergoers and to the pocketbooks of theater concessionaires ever since. Whether motivated by the need to tend to the candles or by the entrepreneurs' wishing to sell oranges and liquor, or both, the indoor theaters eventually established the modern convention of the noncontinuous performance. In the early modern "private" theater, musical performances apparently filled the intermissions, which in Stuart theater jargon seem to have been called "acts."

At the end of the first decade of the seventeenth century, the distinction between public amphitheaters and private indoor companies ceased. For various cultural, political, and economic reasons, individual companies gained control of both the public, open-air theaters and the indoor ones, and companies mixing adult men and boys took over the formerly "private" theaters. Despite the death of the boys' companies and of their highly innovative theaters (for which such luminous playwrights as Ben Jonson, George Chapman, and John Marston wrote), their playing spaces and conventions had an immense impact on subsequent plays: not merely for the intervals (which stressed the artistic and architectonic importance of "acts"), but also because they introduced political and social satire as a popular dramatic ingredient, even in tragedy, and a wider range of actorly effects, encouraged by their more intimate playing spaces.

Even the briefest sketch of the Shakespearean theatrical world would be incomplete without some comment on the social and cultural dimensions of theaters and playing in the period. In an intensely hierarchical and status-conscious society, professional actors and their ventures had hardly any respectability; as we have indicated, to protect themselves against laws designed to curb vagabondage and the increase of masterless men, actors resorted to the near-fiction that they were the servants of noble masters, and wore their distinctive livery. Hence the company for which Shakespeare wrote in the 1590s called itself the Lord Chamberlain's Men and pretended that the public, money-getting performances were in fact rehearsals for private performances before that high court official. From 1598, the Privy Council had licensed theatrical companies, and after 1603, with the accession of King James I, the companies gained explicit royal protection, just as the Queen's Men had for a time under Queen Elizabeth. The Chamberlain's Men became the King's Men, and the other companies were patronized by the other members of the royal family.

These designations were legal fictions that half-concealed an important economic and social development, the evolution away from the theater's organization on the model of the guild, a self-regulating confraternity of individual artisans, into a proto-capitalist organization. Shakespeare's company became a joint-stock company, where persons who supplied capital and, in some cases, such as Shakespeare's, capital and talent, employed themselves and others in earning a return on that capital. This development meant that actors and theater companies were outside both the traditional guild structures, which required some form of civic or royal charter, and the feudal household organization of master-and-servant. This anomalous, maverick social and economic condition made theater companies practically unruly and potentially even dangerous; consequently, numerous official bodies – including the London metropolitan and ecclesiastical authorities as well as, occasionally, the royal court itself – tried, without much success, to control and even to disband them.

Public officials had good reason to want to close the theaters: they were attractive nuisances – they drew often riotous crowds, they were always noisy, and they could be politically offensive and socially insubordinate. Until the Civil War, however, anti-theatrical forces failed to shut down professional theater, for many reasons – limited surveillance and few police powers, tensions or outright hostilities among the agencies that sought to check or channel theatrical activity, and lack of clear policies for control. Another reason must have been the theaters' undeniable popularity. Curtailing any activity enjoyed by such a substantial percentage of the population was difficult, as various Roman emperors attempting to limit circuses had learned, and the Tudor-Stuart audience was not merely large, it was socially diverse and included women. The prevalence of public entertainment in this period has been underestimated. In fact, fairs, holidays, games, sporting events, the equivalent of modern parades, freak shows, and street exhibitions all abounded, but the theater was the most widely and frequently available entertainment to which people of every class had access. That fact helps account both for its quantity and for the fear and anger it aroused.

WILLIAM SHAKESPEARE OF
STRATFORD-UPON-AVON, GENTLEMAN

Many people have said that we know very little about William Shakespeare's life – pinheads and postcards are often mentioned as appropriately tiny surfaces on which to record the available information. More imaginatively and perhaps more correctly, Ralph Waldo Emerson wrote, "Shakespeare is the only biographer of Shakespeare. . . . So far from Shakespeare's being the least known, he is the one person in all modern history fully known to us."

In fact, we know more about Shakespeare's life than we do about almost any other English writer's of his era. His last will and testament (dated March 25, 1616) survives, as do numerous legal contracts and court documents involving Shakespeare as principal or witness, and parish records in Stratford and London. Shakespeare appears quite often in official records of King James's royal court, and of course Shakespeare's name appears on numerous title pages and in the written and recorded words of his literary contemporaries Robert Greene, Henry Chettle, Francis Meres, John Davies of Hereford, Ben Jonson, and many others. Indeed, if we make due allowance for the bloating of modern, run-of-the-mill bureaucratic records, more information has survived over the past four hundred years about William Shakespeare of Stratford-upon-Avon, Warwickshire, than is likely to survive in the next four hundred years about any reader of these words.

What we do not have are entire categories of information – Shakespeare's private letters or diaries, drafts and revisions of poems and plays, critical prefaces or essays, commendatory verse for other writers' works, or instructions guiding his fellow actors in their performances, for instance – that we imagine would help us understand and appreciate his surviving writings. For all we know, many such data never existed as written records. Many literary and theatrical critics, not knowing what might once have existed, more or less cheerfully accept the situation; some even make a theoretical virtue of it by claiming that such data are irrelevant to understanding and interpreting the plays and poems.

So, what do we know about William Shakespeare, the man responsible for thirty-seven or perhaps more plays, more than 150 sonnets, two lengthy narrative poems, and some shorter poems?

While many families by the name of Shakespeare (or some variant spelling) can be identified in the English Midlands as far back as the twelfth century, it seems likely that the dramatist's grandfather, Richard, moved to Snitterfield, a town not far from Stratford-upon-Avon, sometime before 1529. In Snitterfield, Richard Shakespeare leased farmland from the very wealthy Robert Arden. By 1552, Richard's son John had moved to a large house on Henley Street in Stratford-upon-Avon, the house that stands today as "The Birthplace." In Stratford, John Shakespeare traded as a glover, dealt in wool, and lent money at interest; he also served in a variety of civic posts, including "High Bailiff," the municipality's equivalent of mayor. In 1557, he married Robert Arden's youngest daughter, Mary. Mary and John had four sons – William was the oldest – and four daughters, of whom only Joan outlived her most celebrated sibling. William was baptized (an event entered in the Stratford parish church records) on April 26, 1564, and it has become customary, without any good factual support, to suppose he was born on April 23, which happens to be the feast day of Saint George, patron saint of England, and is also the date on which he died, in 1616. Shakespeare married Anne Hathaway in 1582, when he was eighteen and she was twenty-six; their first child was born five months later. It has been generally assumed that the marriage was enforced and subsequently unhappy, but these are only assumptions; it has been estimated, for instance, that up to one third of Elizabethan brides were pregnant when they married. Anne and William Shakespeare had three children: Susanna, who married a prominent local physician, John Hall; and the twins Hamnet, who died young in 1596, and Judith, who married Thomas Quiney – apparently a rather shady individual. The name Hamnet was unusual but not unique: he and his twin sister were named for their godparents, Shakespeare's neighbors Hamnet and Judith Sadler. Shakespeare's father died in 1601 (the year of *Hamlet*), and Mary Arden Shakespeare died in 1608 (the year of *Coriolanus*). William Shakespeare's last surviving direct descendant was his granddaughter Elizabeth Hall, who died in 1670.

Between the birth of the twins in 1585 and a clear reference to Shakespeare as a practicing London dramatist in Robert Greene's sensationalizing, satiric pamphlet, *Greene's Groatsworth of Wit* (1592), there is no record of where William Shakespeare was or what he was doing. These seven so-called lost years have been imaginatively filled by scholars and other students of Shakespeare: some think he traveled to Italy, or fought in the Low Countries, or studied law or medicine, or worked as an apprentice actor/writer, and so on to even more fanciful possibilities. Whatever the biographical facts for those "lost" years, Greene's nasty remarks in 1592 testify to professional envy and to the fact that Shakespeare already had a successful career in London. Speaking to his fellow playwrights, Greene warns both generally and specifically:

> . . . trust them [actors] not: for there is an upstart crow, beautified with our feathers, that with his tiger's heart wrapped in a player's hide supposes he is as well able to bombast out a blank verse as the best of you; and being an absolute Johannes Factotum, is in his own conceit the only Shake-scene in a country.

The passage mimics a line from *3 Henry VI* (hence the play must have been performed before Greene wrote) and seems to say that "Shake-scene" is both actor and playwright, a jack-of-all-trades. That same year, Henry Chettle protested Greene's remarks in *Kind-Heart's Dream,* and each of the next two years saw the publication of poems – *Venus and Adonis* and *The Rape of Lucrece,* respectively – publicly ascribed to (and dedicated by) Shakespeare. Early in 1595 he was named one of the senior members of a prominent acting company, the Lord Chamberlain's Men, when they received payment for court performances during the 1594 Christmas season.

Clearly, Shakespeare had achieved both success and reputation in London. In 1596, upon Shakespeare's application, the College of Arms granted his father the now-familiar coat of arms he had taken the first steps to obtain almost twenty years before, and in 1598, John's son – now permitted to call himself "gentleman" – took a 10 percent share in the new Globe playhouse. In 1597, he bought a substantial bourgeois house, called New Place, in Stratford – the garden remains, but Shakespeare's house, several times rebuilt, was torn down in 1759 – and over the next few years Shakespeare spent large sums buying land and making other investments in the town and its environs. Though he worked in London, his family remained in Stratford, and he seems always to have considered Stratford the home he would eventually return to. Something approaching a disinterested appreciation of Shakespeare's popular and professional status appears in Francis Meres's *Palladis Tamia* (1598), a not especially imaginative and perhaps therefore persuasive record of literary reputations. Reviewing contemporary English writers, Meres lists the titles of many of Shakespeare's plays, including one not now known, *Love's Labor's Won,* and praises his "mellifluous & hony-tongued" "sugred Sonnets," which were then circulating in manuscript (they were first collected in 1609). Meres describes Shakespeare as "one of the best" English playwrights of both comedy and tragedy. In *Remains . . . Concerning Britain* (1605),

William Camden – a more authoritative source than the imitative Meres – calls Shakespeare one of the "most pregnant witts of these our times" and joins him with such writers as Chapman, Daniel, Jonson, Marston, and Spenser. During the first decades of the seventeenth century, publishers began to attribute numerous play quartos, including some non-Shakespearean ones, to Shakespeare, either by name or initials, and we may assume that they deemed Shakespeare's name and supposed authorship, true or false, commercially attractive.

For the next ten years or so, various records show Shakespeare's dual career as playwright and man of the theater in London, and as an important local figure in Stratford. In 1608-9 his acting company – designated the "King's Men" soon after King James had succeeded Queen Elizabeth in 1603 – rented, refurbished, and opened a small interior playing space, the Blackfriars theater, in London, and Shakespeare was once again listed as a substantial sharer in the group of proprietors of the playhouse. By May 11, 1612, however, he describes himself as a Stratford resident in a London lawsuit – an indication that he had withdrawn from day-to-day professional activity and returned to the town where he had always had his main financial interests. When Shakespeare bought a substantial residential building in London, the Blackfriars Gatehouse, close to the theater of the same name, on March 10, 1613, he is recorded as William Shakespeare "of Stratford upon Avon in the county of Warwick, gentleman," and he named several London residents as the building's trustees. Still, he continued to participate in theatrical activity: when the new Earl of Rutland needed an allegorical design to bear as a shield, or *impresa,* at the celebration of King James's Accession Day, March 24, 1613, the earl's accountant recorded a payment of 44 shillings to Shakespeare for the device with its motto.

For the last few years of his life, Shakespeare evidently

concentrated his activities in the town of his birth. Most of the final records concern business transactions in Stratford, ending with the notation of his death on April 23, 1616, and burial in Holy Trinity Church, Stratford-upon-Avon.

THE QUESTION OF AUTHORSHIP

The history of ascribing Shakespeare's plays (the poems do not come up so often) to someone else began, as it continues, peculiarly. The earliest published claim that someone else wrote Shakespeare's plays appeared in an 1856 article by Delia Bacon in the American journal *Putnam's Monthly* – although an Englishman, Thomas Wilmot, had shared his doubts in private (even secretive) conversations with friends near the end of the eighteenth century. Bacon's was a sad personal history that ended in madness and poverty, but the year after her article, she published, with great difficulty and the bemused assistance of Nathaniel Hawthorne (then United States Consul in Liverpool, England), her *Philosophy of the Plays of Shakspere Unfolded*. This huge, ornately written, confusing farrago is almost unreadable; sometimes its intents, to say nothing of its arguments, disappear entirely beneath near-raving, ecstatic writing. Tumbled in with much supposed "philosophy" appear the claims that Francis Bacon (from whom Delia Bacon eventually claimed descent), Walter Ralegh, and several other contemporaries of Shakespeare's had written the plays. The book had little impact except as a ridiculed curiosity.

Once proposed, however, the issue gained momentum among people whose conviction was the greater in proportion to their ignorance of sixteenth- and seventeenth-century English literature, history, and society. Another American amateur, Catherine P. Ashmead Windle, made the next influential contribution to the cause when she published *Report to the British Museum* (1882), wherein she promised to open "the Cipher of Francis Bacon," though what she mostly offers, in the words of S. Schoenbaum, is "demented allegorizing." An entire new cottage industry grew from Windle's suggestion that the texts contain hidden, cryptographically discoverable ciphers – "clues" – to their authorship; and today there are not only books devoted to the putative ciphers, but also pamphlets, journals, and newsletters.

Although Baconians have led the pack of those seeking a substitute Shakespeare, in *"Shakespeare" Identified* (1920), J. Thomas Looney became the first published "Oxfordian" when he proposed Edward de Vere, seventeenth earl of Oxford, as the secret author of Shakespeare's plays. Also for Oxford and his "authorship" there are today dedicated societies, articles, journals, and books. Less popular candidates – Queen Elizabeth and Christopher Marlowe among them – have had adherents, but the movement seems to have divided into two main contending factions, Baconian and Oxfordian. (For further details on all the candidates for "Shakespeare," see S. Schoenbaum, *Shakespeare's Lives,* 2nd ed., 1991.)

The Baconians, the Oxfordians, and supporters of other candidates have one trait in common – they are snobs. Every pro-Bacon or pro-Oxford tract sooner or later claims that the historical William Shakespeare of Stratford-upon-Avon could not have written the plays because he could not have had the training, the university education, the experience, and indeed the imagination or background their author supposedly possessed. Only a learned genius like Bacon or an aristocrat like Oxford could have written such fine plays. (As it happens, lucky male children of the middle class had access to better education than most aristocrats in Elizabethan England – and Oxford was not particularly well educated.) Shakespeare received in the Stratford grammar school a formal education that would daunt many college graduates today; and popular rival playwrights such as the very learned Ben Jonson and George Chapman, both of whom also lacked university training, achieved great artistic success, without being taken as Bacon or Oxford.

Besides snobbery, one other quality characterizes the authorship controversy: lack of evidence. A great deal of testimony from Shakespeare's time shows that Shakespeare wrote Shakespeare's plays and that his contemporaries recognized them as distinctive and distinctly superior. (Some of that contemporary evidence is collected in E. K. Chambers, *William Shakespeare: A Study of Facts and Problems,* 2 vols., 1930.) Since that testimony comes from Shakespeare's enemies and theatrical competitors as well as from his co-workers and from the Elizabethan equivalent of literary journalists, it seems unlikely that, if any one of these sources had known he was a fraud, they would have failed to record that fact.

Books About Shakespeare's Theater

Useful scholarly studies of theatrical life in Shakespeare's day include: G. E. Bentley, *The Jacobean and Caroline Stage,* 7 vols. (1941-68), and the same author's *The Professions of Dramatist and Player in Shakespeare's Time, 1590-1642* (1986); E. K. Chambers, *The Elizabethan Stage,* 4 vols. (1923); R. A. Foakes, *Illustrations of the English Stage, 1580-1642* (1985); Andrew Gurr, *The Shakespearean Stage,* 3rd ed. (1992), and the same author's *Play-going in Shakespeare's London,* 2nd ed. (1996); Edwin Nungezer, *A Dictionary of Actors* (1929); Carol Chillington Rutter, ed., *Documents of the Rose Playhouse* (1984).

Books About Shakespeare's Life

The following books provide scholarly, documented accounts of Shakespeare's life: G. E. Bentley, *Shakespeare: A Biographical Handbook* (1961); E. K. Chambers, *William Shakespeare: A Study of Facts and Problems,* 2 vols. (1930); S. Schoenbaum, *William Shakespeare: A Compact*

Documentary Life (1977); and *Shakespeare's Lives,* 2nd ed. (1991), by the same author. Many scholarly editions of Shakespeare's complete works print brief compilations of essential dates and events. References to Shakespeare's works up to 1700 are collected in C. M. Ingleby et al., *The Shakespeare Allusion-Book,* rev. ed., 2 vols. (1932).

The Texts of Shakespeare

As FAR AS WE KNOW, only one manuscript conceivably in Shakespeare's own hand may (and even this is much disputed) exist: a few pages of a play called *Sir Thomas More,* which apparently was never performed. What we do have, as later readers, performers, scholars, students, are printed texts. The earliest of these survive in two forms: quartos and folios. Quartos (from the Latin for "four") are small books, printed on sheets of paper that were then folded in fours, to make eight double-sided pages. When these were bound together, the result was a squarish, eminently portable volume that sold for the relatively small sum of sixpence (translating in modern terms to about $5.00). In folios, on the other hand, the sheets are folded only once, in half, producing large, impressive volumes taller than they are wide. This was the format for important works of philosophy, science, theology, and literature (the major precedent for a folio Shakespeare was Ben Jonson's *Works,* 1616). The decision to print the works of a popular playwright in folio is an indication of how far up on the social scale the theatrical profession had come during Shakespeare's lifetime. The Shakespeare folio was an expensive book, selling for between fifteen and eighteen shillings, depending on the binding (in modern terms, from about $150 to $180). Twenty Shakespeare plays of the thirty-seven that survive first appeared in quarto, seventeen of which appeared during Shakespeare's lifetime; the rest of the plays are found only in folio.

The First Folio was published in 1623, seven years after Shakespeare's death, and was authorized by his fellow actors, the co-owners of the King's Men. This publication was certainly a mark of the company's enormous respect for Shakespeare; but it was also a way of turning the old plays, most of which were no longer current in the playhouse, into ready money (the folio includes only Shakespeare's plays, not his sonnets or other nondramatic verse). Whatever the motives behind the publication of the folio, the texts it preserves constitute the basis for almost all later editions of the playwright's works. The texts, however, differ from those of the earlier quartos, sometimes in minor respects but often significantly – most strikingly in the two texts of *King Lear,* but also in important ways in *Hamlet, Othello,* and *Troilus and Cressida.* (The variants are recorded in the textual notes to each play in the new Pelican series.) The differences in these texts represent, in a sense, the essence of theater: the texts of plays were initially not intended for publication. They were scripts, designed for the actors to perform – the principal life of the play at this period was in performance. And it follows that in Shakespeare's theater the playwright typically had no say either in how his play was performed or in the disposition of his text – he was an employee of the company. The authoritative figures in the theatrical enterprise were the shareholders in the company, who were for the most part the major actors. They decided what plays were to be done; they hired the playwright and often gave him an outline of the play they wanted him to write. Often, too, the play was a collaboration: the company would retain a group of writers, and parcel out the scenes among them. The resulting script was then the property of the company, and the actors would revise it as they saw fit during the course of putting it on stage. The resulting text belonged to the company. The playwright had no rights in it once he had been paid. (This system survives largely intact in the movie industry, and most of the playwrights of Shakespeare's time were as anonymous as most screenwriters are today.) The script could also, of course, continue to change as the tastes of audiences and the requirements of the actors changed. Many – perhaps most – plays were revised when they were reintroduced after any substantial absence from the repertory, or when they were performed by a company different from the one that originally commissioned the play.

Shakespeare was an exceptional figure in this world because he was not only a shareholder and actor in his company, but also its leading playwright – he was literally his own boss. He had, moreover, little interest in the publication of his plays, and even those that appeared during his lifetime with the authorization of the company show no signs of any editorial concern on the part of the author. Theater was, for Shakespeare, a fluid and supremely responsive medium – the very opposite of the great classic canonical text that has embodied his works since 1623.

The very fluidity of the original texts, however, has meant that Shakespeare has always had to be edited. Here is an example of how problematic the editorial project inevitably is, a passage from the most famous speech in *Romeo and Juliet,* Juliet's balcony soliloquy beginning "O Romeo, Romeo, wherefore art thou Romeo?" Since the eighteenth century, the standard modern text has read,

> What's Montague? It is nor hand, nor foot,
> Nor arm, nor face, nor any other part
> Belonging to a man. O be some other name!
> What's in a name? That which we call a rose
> By any other name would smell as sweet.
> (II.2.40-44)

Editors have three early texts of this play to work from, two quarto texts and the folio. Here is how the First Quarto (1597) reads:

> Whats *Mountague?* It is nor hand nor foote,
> Nor arme, nor face, nor any other part.
> Whats in a name? That which we call a Rofe,
> By any other name would fmell as fweet:

Here is the Second Quarto (1599):

> Whats *Mountague?* it is nor hand nor foote,
> Nor arme nor face, ô be fome other name
> Belonging to a man.
> Whats in a name that which we call a rofe,
> By any other word would fmell as fweete,

And here is the First Folio (1623):

> What's *Mountague?* it is nor hand nor foote,
> Nor arme, nor face, O be fome other name
> Belonging to a man.
> What? in a names that which we call a Rofe,
> By any other word would fmell as fweete,

There is in fact no early text that reads as our modern text does – and this is the most famous speech in the play. Instead, we have three quite different texts, all of which are clearly some version of the same speech, but none of which seems to us a final or satisfactory version. The transcendently beautiful passage in modern editions is an editorial invention: editors have succeeded in conflating and revising the three versions into something we recognize as great poetry. Is this what Shakespeare "really" wrote? Who can say? What we can say is that Shakespeare always had performance, not a book, in mind.

Books About the Shakespeare Texts

The standard study of the printing history of the First Folio is W. W. Greg, *The Shakespeare First Folio* (1955). J. K. Walton, *The Quarto Copy for the First Folio of Shakespeare*

(1971), is a useful survey of the relation of the quartos to the folio. The second edition of Charlton Hinman's *Norton Facsimile* of the First Folio (1996), with a new introduction by Peter Blayney, is indispensable. Stanley Wells and Gary Taylor, *William Shakespeare: A Textual Companion,* keyed to the Oxford text, gives a comprehensive survey of the editorial situation for all the plays and poems.

THE GENERAL EDITORS

Introduction

IN SHAKESPEARE'S *Richard II,* King Richard replies to the English rebels who challenge his power by saying, "The breath of worldly men cannot depose / The deputy elected by the Lord" (III.2.56-57). In Richard's view, the divinely appointed king cannot lawfully be removed by his subjects. Indeed, as Richard sees it, his subjects cannot remove him lawfully or otherwise: no power on earth can do so. He is mistaken, of course, since he is deposed later in the play, but the position he claims as God's deputy was still the one generally claimed for kings and queens in the English monarchical theory of Shakespeare's time.

That position was asserted by King James I, the English ruler at the time *Measure for Measure* was written. Even before James came to power in 1603, he had polemically restated the case for divinely sanctioned royal authority in two books, *The True Law of Free Monarchies* (1598) and *Basilikon Doron* (1599). Both books were reissued in 1603, at the time of James's accession; the first recorded performance of *Measure for Measure* took place, almost concurrently, in 1604. Some lines from the introductory sonnet to *Basilikon Doron,* a book James couched as advice to his son and heir, Prince Henry, bear repetition in the context of *Measure for Measure:*

> If then ye would enjoy a happy reign
> Observe the statutes of your heavenly king,
> And from his law make all your laws to spring.
> Since his lieutenant here ye should remain,
> Reward the just; be steadfast, true and plain.

The nature and power of the lieutenant, or "deputy," as *Measure for Measure* has it, became the subject of prolonged, often ironic, exploration in Shakespeare's play.

Admittedly, the city of Vienna in *Measure for Measure* is no kingdom ruled over by an absolute monarch. Nor, for that matter, is it a Protestant realm, as was Shakespeare's England. It is a Catholic dukedom, and the clerical figures who move through it, including the duke when he goes into disguise, are friars. Yet Shakespeare makes little attempt at strict portrayal of a Viennese or a Catholic world. The suburbs where some brothels in the play are located belong to the geography of Shakespeare's London; there, "suburbs" were areas beyond city jurisdiction in which brothels could flourish – and so could theaters, including Shakespeare's – as they could not under strict city prohibition. Similarly, the play's exploration of "government" (I.1.3) belongs to Shakespeare's own time and place, as does its representation of a seamy, disease-ridden society. Certainly, the duke's understanding and exercise of power remain very close to those of James I's wished-for absolute monarchy. Although the duke begins the play by brushing aside abstract discussion of the "properties" (I.1.3) of government, those properties are precisely what the play will investigate.

When meditating on the character of the good ruler, for example, the duke says, "He who the sword of heaven will bear / Should be as holy as severe" (III.2.249-50). The bearer of heaven's sword is still god's deputy elect. Yet the duke in *Measure for Measure* feels sufficiently uncomfortable in his role as god's deputy to withdraw and deputize someone else in his place. The chosen deputy's deputy is Angelo, whose holy and severe demeanor recommends him. In the course of the play, Angelo deputizes Escalus in turn to execute some of his functions. Yet the duke is skeptical enough about pious appearances to retain control behind the scenes. He thereby places Angelo unwittingly on trial while reserving and masking his own position as deputy. It is from the duke's deputization of his own authority that the play's complicated action arises; the same act of deputization makes *Measure for Measure* a fascinating dramatized experiment in government by deputy. The mechanism under which any legitimate exercise of political and moral authority depends on a chain of "deputies," ultimately authorized by God as the supreme lawgiver, gets put to the test in *Measure for Measure*.

Of course, government works very differently in modern constitutional democracies from the way it worked in Shakespeare's England. Constitutional separations between church and state as well as legal distinctions between public and private domains had barely been instituted in Shakespeare's political world. Yet many of the questions posed in *Measure for Measure* about the nature and limits of state intervention and about the role(s) of those deputized to enforce the law remain current. In fact, late-twentieth-century readers continue to find *Measure for Measure* illuminating, not just about the general difficulty of legislating sexual morality, but about such matters as sexual harassment and blackmail by those in power. One of the play's central incidents – and, as we know, a persistent problem of "government" – concerns the powerful Angelo's offer to trade the condemned Claudio's life for sexual favors from Isabella. When Isabella threatens to expose him, Angelo confidently retorts, "Who will believe thee, Isabel?" (II.4.153). His high position will protect him, and his stainless reputation will make Isabella's charges seem incredible. It will be his word against hers. (Some recent criticism has addressed the severe penalties for "slander" that women invited if they chose to press charges of sexual impropriety against well-placed men during Shakespeare's time; in *Measure for Measure,* however, the "slanders" of which Angelo publicly accuses Isabella are vindicated when the duke exposes him.) What is unusual about the situation in the play is that we are able to witness an exchange of the kind to which there are seldom witnesses in real life. We know the truth about what happened; Angelo is clearly guilty as charged. Any general cultural predisposition to believe the powerful man rather than the woman under such circumstances is thus challenged by the play. Recognition of the play's continuing pertinence has, however, sometimes made *Measure for Measure* seem frustrating rather than satisfying to modern readers and audiences.

Rather than provide general philosophical solutions to the problems it poses, *Measure for Measure* delivers dramatic resolutions plotted according to Elizabethan conventions of romantic comedy ending in marriage. To many modern readers, the comedic happy ending of *Measure for Measure* evades the great issues of the play instead of resolving them in principle. Moreover, the play's grand finale, with marriages all round, has seemed forced, trivializing, problematic, or even sordid to many. For one of the characters, Lucio, forced marriage to a prostitute he has impregnated is a disgusting punishment – a fate worse than death – rather than a romantic reward. Whether marriage will amount to reward or punishment for the other couples involved remains uncertain. Perhaps, however, the play's forced and ambiguous resolution underlines the old dramatic truism that only God can write Act V. Although this duke *plays* God more than most stage characters do, and takes over the plotting of the play (perhaps that is one implication of being God's deputy), the solutions he delivers are no less flawed, theatrical, and conventional than he is. Not even the eye-for-an-eye poetic justice some readers crave is forthcoming. Angelo, who is practically condemned out of his own mouth and pleads for death, is "saved" instead for marriage by Mariana, whom he has previously repudiated. The play's happy ending is far removed from a perfect ending.

An uneasy fit between the dark, philosophical grandeur of *Measure for Measure* and comic devices some moderns have found disconcertingly cheap partly explains the play's classification in the twentieth century as a "problem comedy." (We have no evidence that Shakespeare's contemporaries would have regarded it as a problem.) Deputization, which seems central to the play's most serious concerns, reappears in seemingly frivolous contexts and parodic guises that some readers have found hard to take. Informal "deputization" in the play includes the duke's substitution of Mariana for Isabella in Angelo's bed (the time-honored bed trick of comedy) and the substitution of the dead pirate Ragozine's head for Claudio's. It includes the duke's substitution of yet another self for his own when he goes into disguise as a friar, a disguise in which he can undertake further impersonations, not the least of which is the impersonation of Death. (The fragmentation of the duke into other selves, and the consequent multiplication of his roles, defeats any attempt at integral character analysis.) Substitution – and substitutability – thus seems to emerge as the rule of the play. Why does it do so?

At least a part of the answer is that substitution is the general rule of theater. Actors are substituted for dramatic characters; men (or boy actors) for women, and vice versa; the dead for the living, and vice versa; sexual partners for one another; political functionaries for one another as well as for God. Alone among the characters in *Measure for Measure* (all of whom regard him as practically subhuman), the frequently dead-drunk Barnardine unwittingly resists the general rule of substitution when he refuses to be executed, thus withholding his head as a substitute for Claudio's. Yet even his surly refusal is circumvented when the head of a dead pirate is substituted for the one he declines to give up. In short, it is to a general rule of substitution that *Measure for Measure* owes its very existence as a play, and it is under the same rule that it produces its full range of effects, whether they strike us as dissonant or not. (Current "postmodern" readers and viewers of the play may in fact be more tolerant of dissonance, discrepancy, and parody than ones earlier in this century.) Where "all the world's a stage," as Jaques puts it in Shakespeare's *As You Like It,* substitution will be the rule.

The prehistory of the specific case to be considered under this general rule is outlined, mainly by the duke, at the beginning of the play. We are told that the citizens of Vienna, too long accustomed to lax regulation, have become morally dissolute and sexually licentious. The duke wishes to reimpose strict order, yet he feels that, having allowed things to slip, he cannot cruelly rein in his subjects himself. In this respect, the play echoes some of the language of *Basilikon Doron.* Warning against beginning a reign too tolerantly, James wrote, "And when ye have by the severity of justice once settled your countries, and made them know that ye can strike, then may ye after all the days of your life mix justice with mercy . . . for if otherwise ye kith [make known] your clemency at the first, the offenses would soon come to such great heaps [that you] against your nature would be compelled to wrack many whom the chastisement of few in the beginning might have preserved."* Shakespeare's duke accordingly appoints the austere Angelo to curb the citizens, investing him with full ducal powers. The duke then withdraws, ostensibly on a foreign mission but actually to become a disguised onlooker and manipulator of Angelo's rule.

Age-old questions about the appropriate degree of sexual regulation in society and about the relation between social and sexual order are thus implicitly raised at the beginning of the play. The implied norm to be policed under Angelo's rule is that of heterosexual marriage and procreation as the sole legitimate avenue of human sexuality. The first transgressor of whom Angelo decides to make an example is accordingly a young man, Claudio,

* James I, *Basilikon Doron,* ed. C. H. McIlwain (Cambridge: Harvard University Press, 1918): 20.

who has impregnated a young woman, Juliet, to whom he is only betrothed, not yet married. In sentencing Claudio to death, as Viennese law allows him to do, Angelo imposes a penalty that is not just unprecedented under the duke's rule but seems outrageously excessive to practically everyone but Angelo. For Angelo, however, enforcing the letter of the law – to which he believes he adheres in his own life – is the only way to begin an effective reform. Simultaneously with sentencing Claudio, Angelo attempts to close down all the Viennese brothels and severely penalize prostitutes and pimps. Angelo thus evidently regards organized prostitution as a cause and symptom of the same moral laxity for which Claudio is to be punished, and as a similar threat to marriage.

Ostensibly, Angelo's strict enforcement will uphold biblically prescribed moral and social norms, and will revive a respect for law and order that has been eroded through "liberty" (I.2.124). In other words, it will instill new terror into enforcement, needed to render the law effective. Angelo's enforcement may less overtly and perhaps only subconsciously be intended to promote public hygiene by limiting the spread of sexually transmitted disease, obviously rampant in Vienna. Yet we soon begin to glimpse Angelo's difficulties. Elbow the constable is a bumbling incompetent. Escalus, Angelo's deputy, is well-meaning but ineffectual. More damaging to Angelo's prospects, we learn, is the fact that brothels in the city, unlike those in the suburbs, have been saved by the intervention of a "wise burgher" (I.2.99). A political limit to Angelo's moral reform thus becomes evident; so does the fact that sex is a profitable free-market commodity with its own specialized providers. Public policy driven by moral concerns alone cannot overcome these brute facts. Moreover, when the bawd Pompey learns of Angelo's new policy of strict enforcement, he remarks that Angelo will have "to geld and splay all the youth of the city" (II.1.219-20). In

effect, Pompey is making the self-serving claim that brothels cater to the uncontrollable lust of young men, yet he
has a point: not even savage penalties are enough to con-
fine all youthful sexual activities within the bounds of
marriage. The unavailing savagery of the penalties may in
turn promote disrespect for the law. So must the transfor-
mation of Pompey the bawd into an agent of the law
when he is made assistant hangman. Ironically, Angelo
himself will become the play's prime example of lawless-
ness. Unexpectedly succumbing to his own desire for Isabella, he will become the corrupter of the very law he has
been deputized to uphold. All in all, Angelo's reforms
have a great deal more to contend with than he antici-
pates.

Measure for Measure, then, seriously addresses issues of
justice and law enforcement. Characters in the play, no-
tably Angelo and Isabella, debate the issues with remark-
able passion and eloquence. Yet the play as a whole reveals
the huge gap between godlike aspirations and fallible
human implementation. Indeed, the play goes further
than I have already hinted in getting *behind* the wish for
moral reform that drives the action. We are prompted to
consider whether, or to what extent, the characters' moral
rhetoric actually rationalizes and masks barely conscious
sexual phobias arising from many causes: for example,
from people's uneasy relation to their own sexuality (both
its intensity and its "lawless" orientations); from the
seemingly unbreakable link between human sexuality and
human mortality (a connection underlined by jocular yet
obsessive allusion in the play to sexually transmitted diseases); from various forms of sexual threat or abuse; from
the deep sense of guilt regarding sex instilled by Christian
tradition (even Claudio, who does not believe he has done
anything terrible in impregnating Juliet, nevertheless feels
sinful enough to reconcile himself, at moments, to a
death sentence). All these phobia-inducing circumstances
are sufficiently evident in the play to hint at an undercur-

rent of panic in its agendas of moral reform. Correspond-
ingly, the play invites us to consider to what extent the in-
crimination of sexual offenders is a form of scapegoating
for social and sexual "disorders" that can never fully be
brought under control.

The institution of the prison in Vienna powerfully ex-
emplifies both the penal impulse in the play and its limits.
The existence of the prison implies a wish on the part of
the authorities to cordon off – or internally exile – all
threats to good order. Yet oscillation in the play between
the social world of Vienna and its prison world reveals a
failure to achieve this separation. The organized social
world of the prison becomes an ironic reflection of the society in which it is situated, and a number of the characters cross the boundary between the two with only a
change of role or costume. The social and prison worlds
become increasingly interdependent, and the solution to
the problems of the play depends on the mobility of characters across the supposedly dividing line.

Whatever we think of the solutions found in the play,
they cannot possibly encompass all the circumstances, including unconscious ones, to which they respond. Such,
perhaps, is one conclusion to be drawn from Shakespeare's study of "government," a term that increasingly
throughout the play encompasses personal issues as well
as explicitly political ones. Indeed, questions of public
order and individual self-government remain interrelated
throughout the play. When we first meet Isabella, she is
seeking to enter a nunnery in which she can preserve her
chastity and submit to regulation far stricter than that
prevailing in Vienna (she even finds the convent rule
somewhat too liberal for her taste). Her desire to enter the
convent is an implied comment on the laxity of the Viennese social world and on the tainted selves – both bodies
and souls – that it produces. The convent itself represents
an attempt to cordon off an area of (female) purity from
the contaminated city; what Isabella proposes for herself

is internal exile from Vienna in a community of pure, strict, self-governing women. Her choosing to submit to strict discipline is an implicit defense of her inviolate selfhood, not just against the dissoluteness of the city, in which prostitution is rampant, but from lawful, patriarchal marriage as a threat to women's autonomy and bodily intactness. Beyond even these motivations, the play suggests that Isabella's flight to the convent also represents an attempt on her part to separate herself from her brother Claudio, for whom she manifestly retains some incestuous sibling desire. Isabella's wish to enter the convent thus includes a phobic element of which she seems unaware; to feel secure, she wishes to substitute pure "sisterhood" (I.4.5) for the cross-gendered sibling relation. Isabella's retreat will soon be thwarted in the play when Lucio, who makes his way into the convent, urges her to plead with Angelo on behalf of Claudio. Isabella is thus drawn back into the world of compromising relationships, ultimately including marriage to the duke. Her concern for Claudio notwithstanding, Isabella's willingness to emerge from the convent she has just joined implies some ambivalence on her part about the cloistered life she has chosen.

Drawing on contemporary contexts, *Measure for Measure* supplies a particularly rich commentary on Isabella's impulse to withdraw. Although Catholicism continued to uphold ideals of chastity and cloistered virtue in Shakespeare's time, those ideals were relentlessly attacked and discredited by mainstream Protestants in England. In fact, English Catholic monasteries and convents had been dissolved during the reign of Henry VIII, while church property had been confiscated by the state. Virtuous marriage and procreation rather than celibate withdrawal were upheld as ideals for both men and women, though a double standard prevailed: more toleration was extended to men's transgressions. Isabella's initial decision to join a convent would have been regarded as questionable by many of Shakespeare's contemporaries; when the duke proposes marriage to her at the end of the play, he is offering her the "right" Protestant choice. (Different eras have responded differently to the fact that the text gives her no line accepting the offer, and in modern productions she has even occasionally refused it.)

The great English Puritan poet John Milton, in *Areopagitica,* definitively stated the English Protestant case in the seventeenth century. There, Milton discredited what he called "a fugitive and cloistered virtue," adding that "we bring not innocence into this world, we bring impurity much rather." In other words, the selves – and bodies – we would protect by walling out impurity already carry impurity within them; such is the meaning of original sin. The same point is graphically made in a poem called "Upon Appleton House" by Milton's contemporary Andrew Marvell; there, the Catholic nunnery is recalled as a fortified setting in which female vice and self-indulgence can flourish. Yet despite the force and persistence of the Protestant attack, cloistral ideals and impulses died hard. A long Catholic tradition did not end overnight in Protestant England. English Puritanism represented an attempt to redefine rather than wholly discredit religious aspirations to purity. Moreover, for both women and men, but perhaps more importantly for women, the cloistered life represented a rational alternative to the coercive norm of patriarchal marriage as well as to the sexual marketplace. This rational choice would no doubt have been phobically reinforced. Submitting to the rule of cloistered chastity (a choice sometimes entailing the rigors and ecstasies of martyrdom) was a paradoxical way of reclaiming self-determination in a "place apart." Shakespeare was not dealing with dead issues in *Measure for Measure.*

If Isabella represents the impulse to seek out a haven from the social world of the city, Mariana represents the corresponding danger to women of finding themselves relegated to an unchosen place apart. We hear that Mariana had been betrothed to Angelo, yet he had repudiated her when her dowry failed to come up to expectations. He additionally claims that her reputation had been tainted by rumors of sexual misconduct. She was therefore no longer fit to be his bride. Mariana is thus excluded from the marriage market, in which women's only opportunity for social inclusion resides, and she is confined to a "moated grange" (III.1.262), a place of exile from the life of the city. Mariana is the exemplary victim of a world in which adult single women have no place. Her isolation, which threatens to be perpetual, in a country house *outside* the city, makes the point. The duke recalls her only when she is needed as a substitute for Isabella in Angelo's bed: otherwise, she would forever be relegated to solitary uselessness. Shakespeare invests the injured Mariana with a gentle dignity and inwardness that captured the imagination of Victorian readers, yet her eventual plea to marry Angelo, instead of getting even with him when she has the opportunity, implies that a nonreligious woman's only alternative to marriage in Vienna is social death. Although the duke offers to invest her with Angelo's property when he is executed, thus enabling her to "buy" (V.1.423) another husband, her self-respect, along with a perverse, rejected-woman's attachment to him, makes her plead for Angelo's life. She will make do with him.

The polemical charge of Milton's and Marvell's previously cited works, written in the aftermath of a civil war in which the properties of government (I.1.3) had been bloodily disputed on the battlefield, seems absent from Shakespeare's play. Yet both Isabella and Mariana *are* "saved" for marriage through the duke's intervention. Neither Mariana's melancholy self-sufficiency nor Isabella's "fugitive and cloistered virtue" proves tenable in the world of the play. Indeed, the innocence Isabella wishes to maintain becomes subject in the play, and in modern criticism, to interpretations ranging from saintly goodness through simplemindedness to coldness, excessive zeal, seductiveness, and hypocrisy. Far from her own innocence being mirrored by Angelo's, Isabella's innocence tantalizes Angelo and inflames a lust he has never suspected in himself (his own "angelic" innocence thus proves illusory). Whether innocence consists in purity of body and soul from which moral energy flows, or whether it consists in denial, unconsciousness, and even deafness to verbal nuances, is a question constantly posed by the figure of Isabella, both in the play and in subsequent criticism.

"Innocent" and "guilty" meanings are almost inseparably fused in the very language the characters must exchange. When Claudio, for example, asks Lucio to get Isabella to plead for him, he says, "in her youth / There is a prone and speechless dialect, / Such as move men" (I.2.181–83). What this means is that her youthful, feminine helplessness may soften the austere Angelo, yet Isabella's passive sexual body is also already being conceived, however unconsciously, as the "language" most likely to move Angelo. The knowing Lucio, who coaches Isabella, will deliberately exploit her erotic appeal, yet even in her innocence Isabella cannot escape the sexual scenarios embedded in language. When, on her second visit to Angelo, he says, "How now, fair maid!" and she replies, "I am come to know your pleasure" (II.4.30), these perfectly conventional courtesies are innuendo-laden even if neither speaker is conscious of the fact. Innocent intent is not enough to control the effects and implications of the language characters exchange, or to neutralize the erotic charge any statement (or even silence) may take on in a particular context. Any social exchange at all is thus subject to risk. Paradoxically, as Angelo notes, Isabella's innocence operates on him as a more powerful aphrodisiac than would any practiced seductiveness.

Although in different ways, the personal innocence and strict self-government to which Isabella and Angelo aspire crumble in the course of the play. Despite experiencing severe shock and conflict, Angelo succumbs to outright corruption in offering to trade Claudio's life for sex with Isabella. He compounds his guilt by trying to have Claudio executed anyway after Isabella appears to have kept her side of the bargain. Isabella, on the other hand, who retains our respect, becomes party to the somewhat shabby trick in which Mariana is substituted for her in Angelo's bed. Good government, whether public or personal, evidently cannot be predicated on anyone's wholly untarnished innocence.

If this fact becomes clear in the case of Isabella and Angelo, it becomes equally so in the case of the duke. However well-meant his scheme to rectify matters in Vienna, that scheme, which he often seems to be making up as he goes along, depends from the start on deception. He deceives everyone about his intent in leaving the city. In effect, he sets Angelo up for a fall, thus eliciting sympathy for Angelo no matter how badly he behaves. In his disguise as a friar, the duke hoodwinks and manipulates practically everyone. The friar's costume enables him to eavesdrop, hear confessions, and conduct surveillance; even in a good cause, these are the shady arts of political omniscience. His plot to bring about a happy ending not only entails the bed trick but becomes self-serving insofar as he, too, fixes on Isabella, thus making himself Angelo's mirror and rival.

Although there are moments when the duke speaks a language more lofty, oracular, and "inhuman" than that spoken by anyone else in the play, this godlike self-elevation by no means places him above the fray. On the contrary, he seems to regard Lucio's slanders against *him* as more unforgivable than any other crime committed in the play. This personal animus implies that he has been deeply stung by these slanders, the truth or falsity of which we can never fully determine. Yet it is not only the content of the slanders that appears to upset the duke. By going into disguise as a friar, he hears things said about him that he ordinarily would never have heard; such is one risk of assuming a disguise. The duke thus makes the unforeseen discovery that *he*, the ruler, is not immune to gossip and malicious (mis)interpretation. Although he claims that government as such is impaired by irresponsible slander, his vengeful anguish also suggests that he has assumed others see him in the same favorable light as he sees himself. That too is a form of innocence the world will not allow. Even the duke's sexuality, which he denies in his role as friar and presumably wants to keep out of consideration in his exercise of public office, has been a subject of much recent critical speculation, some of it prompted by Lucio's scandalous tales.

If the properties of government are explored in the play, inseparably from the properties of those who govern, so is the condition of the governed, both gentry and commoners. Although Vienna is a class-divided city, a situation that gives rise to both high and low comedy in the play, the sex trade crosses the class divide and seemingly routes all participants to the same destination – namely, the "bath houses" in which mercury vapor is used as a horribly drastic remedy for syphilis. Syphilitic hair loss, disfigurement, and bone decay supply material for countless anxious witticisms in the play, bandied especially among the men-about-town who have good cause to worry. Seeking to ward off the ailment by projecting it onto others seems to be the favored humorous defense mechanism, while calling it "the French disease" implies that it is really foreign to Vienna (or Shakespeare's England). We should recall that syphilis, named by the Italian humanist physician Girolamo Fracastoro in 1530, could still be regarded, mistakenly or otherwise, in Shakespeare's England as a relatively new contagious disease with no safe or reliable cure (the idea of contagion itself being novel). It was certainly seen as representing a threat to the healthy "body politic," and it called into question the age-old medical model under which disease was thought to be caused mainly by humoral imbalances originating inside the body. Like plague before it, and somewhat like AIDS in our own time, epidemic syphilis required that the nature and regulative role of the state be reconsidered. Such forced reflection isn't explicit in *Measure for Measure,* yet syphilis is manifestly one disturbing circumstance to which both governors and governed are reacting in the play.

If sex and death are the great levelers in Vienna (so too is the prison), the sexual marketplace has its own professionals and even mock heroes. The bawd's name Pompey is that of a great Roman general, a fact that produces several jokes at his expense. (Escalus remarks that Pompey's greatness consists, unlike that of his Roman namesake, in the size of his bum, or buttocks, Bum also happening to be this Pompey's vulgar surname.) Modern readers may find it puzzling that the names of legendary Roman generals, Pompey and Caesar, along with that of the Carthaginian leader Hannibal, are rudely bandied about in the Viennese street. A Jacobean debasement of legendary masculine virtue, as well as of the "field" of male action, may be implied by this transposition. We should recall, however, that James I billed himself as a peacemaking king, uniting the kingdom and even trying to outlaw the piracy Englishmen had engaged in with tacit royal sanction during Elizabeth I's reign (the imprisonment of the pirate Ragozine in the play makes the point). Debasement of heroic, warrior masculinity would not necessarily have been inconsistent with James's goals. His own Roman model was the peacemaking, law-giving Augustus Caesar, not the Julius who had ignited the civil wars in Italy. In the play, the mock hero Pompey disturbs the peace and good order of the city. In any event, as an irrepressibly humorous scofflaw and dauntless spokesperson for his trade, Pompey gets short shrift under Angelo's regime; unlike the good-natured, vacillating Escalus,

Angelo does not bandy words with offenders. Nevertheless, it seems unlikely that Angelo's short-lived, self-
deconstructing reform will have much lasting effect. It
would appear that, in its Jacobean context, the play can
end only by staging prospective marriage, however ques-
tionably, as good social policy. That outcome is not without irony given James I's own perceived preference for
men, a preference the duke in *Measure for Measure* has
been suspected by some critics of sharing.

In conclusion, then, why "measure for measure"? For a
long time, critics have recognized the allusion of the play's
title to Matthew 7:1-2, a passage from Christ's Sermon on
the Mount: "Judge not, that ye be not judged. For with
what judgment ye judge, ye shall be judged: and with
what measure ye mete, it shall be measured to you again."
The title phrase, repeated in the play, orients us toward
the biblical horizon of much Jacobean thinking on questions of law and morality; it reminds us as well that
Shakespeare's culture was deeply infused with biblical lore
and citation. To return in conclusion to *Basilikon Doron,*
James wrote that "As ye are a good Christian, so may ye be
a good king . . . a good king, thinking his highest honor
to consist in the due discharge of his calling, employeth
all his study and pains to procure and maintain, by the
making and execution of good laws, the welfare and peace
of his people" (18). With reference to these overlapping
religious and political contexts, critics have often debated
both the quality of the justice the play delivers and its attempt to balance the respective claims of Law and Mercy.
Few critics have argued, however, that the play effectively
closes the gap between biblical precept and social implementation. Perhaps it is the difficulty of doing so that
Measure for Measure highlights above all.

JONATHAN CREWE
Dartmouth College

Note on the Text

MEASURE FOR MEASURE was first printed in the 1623 folio edition of Shakespeare's works. I have followed that text throughout, with only occasional, minor departures. In keeping with this hands-off policy, I have generally adhered to the folio stage directions, even in the few cases where they present problems. There is little about the staging of the play that cannot be left to the initiative of readers and directors. I have, however, followed the scene division of the previous Pelican series editor, R. C. Bald, where that division differs from the folio scene division. I have also incorporated much of Bald's editorial work. The punctuation has been modernized, in keeping with standard practice for the new series. Material departures from the folio text are listed below, with the adopted reading in italics followed by the folio reading in roman.

The Names of All the Actors . . . The Scene: Vienna (printed at the end of the play in F)
I.2 12 *Why,* Why? 133 *morality* mortality
I.3 27 *Becomes* (not in F) 43 *it* in
I.4 54 *givings-out* giving-out 78 *make* makes
II.1 12 *your* our 39 *breaks* brakes 67 *honor* – honour. 70 *woman* – woman.
II.2 58 *back* (not in F) 96 *new* now 99 *ere* here 149 *sicles* Sickles
II.4 9 *seared* feard 52 *or* and 75 *me* (not in F) 93 *all-binding* all-building 126 *Women, help heaven!* Women? Helpe heaven;
III.1 29 *sire* fire 52 *me to hear them* them to heare me 68 *Though* Through 90 *enew* emmew 95 *damnedest* damnest 129 *penury* periury 212 *by* to
III.2 23 *array* away 37 *Free from* From 45 *it* (not in F) 71 *bondage; if* bondage if 144 *dearer* deare 214 *and* and as
IV.1 3 *day,* day 25 *welcome* well come 58 s.d. *Exeunt* Exit
IV.2 56 *yare* Y'are 58 s.d. *Exeunt* Exit 99 *lordship's* Lords 141 *reckless* wreaklesse
IV.3 7 *Marry, then* marrie then, 15 *Forthright* Forthlight 22 *What* . . .

Barnardine! (followed in F by s.d. "Barnardine within.") **88** *yonder*
yond **104** *I'll . . . speed* (followed in F by s.d. "Isabell within.")
IV.4 2 *manner.* manner, **5** *redeliver* reliver **13–16** *Well, I . . . you well*
(prose in F) **24** *off* of **30** *lived* livèd
IV.5 6 *Flavius'* Flavia's
V.1 13 *me your* we our **117** *ripened* ripenèd **169** *her face* your face
182–83 *Silence . . . himself* (prose in F) **226** *affianced* affiancèd **259**
My . . . throughly (prose in F) **304** *unhallowed* unhallowèd **377 s.d.**
Exeunt Exit **421** *confiscation* confutation **444** *governed* governèd
475 s.d. *Juliet* Iulietta **537** *that's* that

Measure for Measure

THE NAMES OF ALL THE ACTORS

VINCENTIO, *the duke*
ANGELO, *the deputy*
ESCALUS, *an ancient lord*
CLAUDIO, *a young gentleman*
LUCIO, *a fantastic*
TWO OTHER LIKE GENTLEMEN
[VARRIUS, *a gentleman attending on the duke*]
PROVOST
[A JUSTICE]
THOMAS ⎱ *two friars*
PETER ⎰
ELBOW, *a simple constable*
FROTH, *a foolish gentleman*
CLOWN *[Pompey]*
ABHORSON, *an executioner*
BARNARDINE, *a dissolute prisoner*
ISABELLA, *sister to Claudio*
MARIANA, *betrothed to Angelo*
JULIET, *beloved of Claudio*
FRANCISCA, *a nun*
MISTRESS OVERDONE, *a bawd*
[LORDS, OFFICERS, CITIZENS, BOY, AND
   ATTENDANTS]

THE SCENE: *Vienna*

*

Measure for Measure

∾ **I.1** *Enter Duke, Escalus, Lords [, and Attendants].*

DUKE   Escalus.
ESCALUS   My lord.
DUKE

    Of government the properties to unfold,   3
    Would seem in me t' affect speech and discourse,   4
    Since I am put to know that your own science   5
    Exceeds, in that, the lists of all advice   6
    My strength can give you. Then no more remains
    But that, to your sufficiency, as your worth is able,   8
    And let them work. The nature of our people,
    Our city's institutions, and the terms   10
    For common justice, you are as pregnant in   11
    As art and practice hath enrichèd any
    That we remember. There is our commission,
    From which we would not have you warp. Call hither,   14
    I say, bid come before us Angelo.   *[Exit an Attendant.]*
    What figure of us think you he will bear?   16
    For you must know, we have with special soul   17
    Elected him our absence to supply,
    Lent him our terror, dressed him with our love,   19

I.1 The palace of Duke Vincentio   **3** *properties* attributes   **4** *t' affect . . . discourse* to love speech-making   **5** *put to know* i.e., do know; *science* knowledge   **6** *lists* limits   **8–9** *But . . . work* (some words or lines missing?)   **10** *terms* legal enactments   **11** *pregnant* well-versed   **14** *warp* deviate   **16** *What . . . bear* i.e., what image of me will he present   **17** *with special soul* after deep consideration   **19** *terror* awesome power

20   And given his deputation all the organs
        Of our own power. What think you of it?
ESCALUS
        If any in Vienna be of worth
23   To undergo such ample grace and honor,
        It is Lord Angelo.
            Enter Angelo.
DUKE   Look where he comes.
ANGELO
        Always obedient to your grace's will,
        I come to know your pleasure.
DUKE   Angelo,
27   There is a kind of character in thy life,
        That to th' observer doth thy history
29   Fully unfold. Thyself and thy belongings
30   Are not thine own so proper, as to waste
        Thyself upon thy virtues, they on thee.
        Heaven doth with us as we with torches do,
        Not light them for themselves; for if our virtues
        Did not go forth of us, 'twere all alike
35   As if we had them not. Spirits are not finely touched
36   But to fine issues, nor nature never lends
37   The smallest scruple of her excellence
38   But like a thrifty goddess she determines
        Herself the glory of a creditor,
40   Both thanks and use. But I do bend my speech
41   To one that can my part in him advertise.
        Hold therefore, Angelo:
43   In our remove be thou at full ourself.
        Mortality and mercy in Vienna

---

20 *deputation* office as deputy; *organs* instruments   **23** *undergo* uphold   **27** *character* readable script   **29** *belongings* attributes   **30** *proper* exclusively   **30–31** *as to waste . . . on thee* i.e., to waste yourself on your own virtues or waste them only on yourself   **35** *finely touched* nobly stirred   **36** *But . . . issues* i.e., unless something fine comes from them   **37** *scruple* minute particle   **38** *determines* awards   **40** *use* interest   **41** *that . . . advertise* i.e., can instruct himself in playing my part   **43** *remove* absence

Live in thy tongue and heart. Old Escalus,
Though first in question, is thy secondary.   46
Take thy commission.
ANGELO   Now, good my lord,
Let there be some more test made of my mettle   48
Before so noble and so great a figure
Be stamped upon it.   50
DUKE   No more evasion.
We have with a leavened and preparèd choice   51
Proceeded to you, therefore take your honors.
Our haste from hence is of so quick condition   53
That it prefers itself, and leaves unquestioned   54
Matters of needful value. We shall write to you,   55
As time and our concernings shall importune,   56
How it goes with us, and do look to know
What doth befall you here. So fare you well:
To th' hopeful execution do I leave you
Of your commissions.   60
ANGELO   Yet give leave, my lord,
That we may bring you something on the way.   61
DUKE
My haste may not admit it.
Nor need you, on mine honor, have to do
With any scruple; your scope is as mine own,   64
So to enforce or qualify the laws   65
As to your soul seems good. Give me your hand.
I'll privily away. I love the people,   67
But do not like to stage me to their eyes.
Though it do well, I do not relish well   69

---

46 *in question* in rank and in my consideration   48 *mettle* worth (punning
on "metal")   50 *stamped* i.e., as on a coin blank   51 *leavened* well-
considered (i.e., yeasted and risen like good bread)   53 *so quick condition* ur-
gent   54 *prefers* takes precedence; *unquestioned* unconsidered   55 *needful
value* pressing importance   56 *concernings . . . importune* concerns require
61 *something* some distance   64 *scruple* hesitation   65 *qualify* mitigate   67
privily secretly   69 *Though . . . do well* even if it is fitting

70 Their loud applause and aves vehement,
71 Nor do I think the man of safe discretion
72 That does affect it. Once more, fare you well.

ANGELO
 The heavens give safety to your purposes!

ESCALUS
 Lead forth and bring you back in happiness!

DUKE
 I thank you; fare you well.   *Exit.*

ESCALUS
 I shall desire you, sir, to give me leave
 To have free speech with you; and it concerns me
78 To look into the bottom of my place.
 A power I have, but of what strength and nature
80 I am not yet instructed.

ANGELO
 'Tis so with me. Let us withdraw together,
82 And we may soon our satisfaction have
 Touching that point.

ESCALUS   I'll wait upon your honor. *Exeunt.*

        ＊

∾ **I.2** *Enter Lucio and two other Gentlemen.*

LUCIO If the duke, with the other dukes, come not to
2 composition with the King of Hungary, why then all
3 the dukes fall upon the king.

FIRST GENTLEMAN Heaven grant us its peace, but not
5 the King of Hungary's!

SECOND GENTLEMAN Amen.

---

70 *aves* salutations 71 *safe discretion* good judgment 72 *affect* like, enjoy
78 *bottom* full extent; *place* power, position 82 *satisfaction* full understanding
 I.2 A street in Vienna 2 *composition* agreement 3 *fall upon* attack, devour
5 *Hungary's* (pun on "hungry")

LUCIO   Thou conclud'st like the sanctimonious pirate,
that went to sea with the Ten Commandments, but
scraped one out of the table.   9

SECOND GENTLEMAN   "Thou shalt not steal"?   10

LUCIO   Ay, that he razed.   11

FIRST GENTLEMAN   Why, 'twas a commandment to command the captain and all the rest from their functions: 13
they put forth to steal. There's not a soldier of us all
that, in the thanksgiving before meat, do relish the pe-
tition well that prays for peace.

SECOND GENTLEMAN   I never heard any soldier dislike it.

LUCIO   I believe thee, for I think thou never wast where
grace was said.

SECOND GENTLEMAN   No? A dozen times at least.   20

FIRST GENTLEMAN   What? In meter?   21

LUCIO   In any proportion or in any language.   22

FIRST GENTLEMAN   I think, or in any religion.

LUCIO   Ay, why not? Grace is grace, despite of all contro-   24
versy: as, for example, thou thyself art a wicked villain,
despite of all grace.

SECOND GENTLEMAN   Well, there went but a pair of   27
shears between us.

LUCIO   I grant, as there may between the lists and the   29
velvet. Thou art the list.   30

FIRST GENTLEMAN   And thou the velvet. Thou art good   31
velvet; thou'rt a three-piled piece, I warrant thee. I had
as lief be a list of an English kersey as be piled, as thou   33
art piled, for a French velvet. Do I speak feelingly now?   34

---

9 *table* tablet   11 *razed* erased   13 *functions* occupations   21 *in meter* i.e., a
rhyming grace   22 *proportion* (poetic) form   24–26 *Grace . . . grace* (wordplay on *grace* as divine gift and a prayer before a meal)   27–28 *there went . . .
us* i.e., we are cut from the same cloth   29 *lists* the plain edges of fancy velvet cloth   31–34 *Thou . . . velvet* (wordplay on *piled* as the nap of *velvet* and
"pilled" as plucked threadbare, the latter in reference to hair loss through
syphilis – the "*French* disease")   33 *kersey* plain, homespun cloth   34 *feelingly* eloquently

35 LUCIO   I think thou dost, and indeed with most painful
feeling of thy speech. I will, out of thine own confes-
37 sion, learn to begin thy health, but, whilst I live, forget
to drink after thee.

39 FIRST GENTLEMAN   I think I have done myself wrong,
40 have I not?

SECOND GENTLEMAN   Yes, that thou hast, whether thou
42 art tainted or free.

Enter Bawd [Mistress Overdone].

43 LUCIO   Behold, behold, where Madam Mitigation comes!
I have purchased as many diseases under her roof as
come to —

SECOND GENTLEMAN   To what, I pray?

LUCIO   Judge.

48 SECOND GENTLEMAN   To three thousand dolors a year.

FIRST GENTLEMAN   Ay, and more.

50 LUCIO   A French crown more.

51 FIRST GENTLEMAN   Thou art always figuring diseases in
me, but thou art full of error. I am sound.

LUCIO   Nay, not — as one would say — healthy, but so
54 sound as things that are hollow. Thy bones are hollow;
55 impiety has made a feast of thee.

FIRST GENTLEMAN   How now, which of your hips has the
57 most profound sciatica?

MISTRESS OVERDONE   Well, well. There's one yonder arrested and carried to prison was worth five thousand of
60 you all.

35–36 *painful feeling* i.e., syphilitic sores make speaking painful 37
learn . . . health i.e., like a priest, teach you better   37–38 *forget . . . thee* i.e.,
I'll drink to your health, but not from the same cup (for fear of infection)
39 *done myself wrong* i.e., embarrassingly set myself up for your jibes   42
tainted or free infected or free from infection   43 *Madam Mitigation* (so addressed because as prostitute and brothel keeper she "mitigates" men's desires)   48 *dolors* pains (punning on "dollars")   50 *French crown* (1) gold
coin, (2) bald head caused by syphilis   51 *figuring* imagining   54 *bones . . .
hollow* i.e., consumed by venereal disease   55 *impiety* bad conduct   57 *profound sciatica* i.e., deepest pain

SECOND GENTLEMAN   Who's that, I pray thee?

MISTRESS OVERDONE   Marry, sir, that's Claudio, Signor
Claudio.

FIRST GENTLEMAN   Claudio to prison? 'Tis not so.

MISTRESS OVERDONE   Nay, but I know 'tis so. I saw him
arrested, saw him carried away, and, which is more,
within these three days his head to be chopped off.

LUCIO   But, after all this fooling, I would not have it so.
Art thou sure of this?

MISTRESS OVERDONE   I am too sure of it, and it is for get- 70
ting Madam Julietta with child.

LUCIO   Believe me, this may be. He promised to meet
me two hours since, and he was ever precise in promise- 73
keeping.

SECOND GENTLEMAN   Besides, you know, it draws something near to the speech we had to such a purpose.

FIRST GENTLEMAN   But most of all, agreeing with the
proclamation.

LUCIO   Away, let's go learn the truth of it.
                            Exit [Lucio with the Gentlemen].

MISTRESS OVERDONE   Thus what with the war, what 80
with the sweat, what with the gallows, and what with 81
poverty, I am custom-shrunk. 82
        Enter Clown [Pompey].
How now? What's the news with you?

POMPEY   Yonder man is carried to prison.

MISTRESS OVERDONE   Well, what has he done?

POMPEY   A woman.

MISTRESS OVERDONE   But what's his offense?

POMPEY   Groping for trouts in a peculiar river. 88

MISTRESS OVERDONE   What? Is there a maid with child
by him? 90

---

73 *precise* punctilious   81 *sweat* sweating sickness   82 *custom-shrunk* short
of customers   88 *Groping . . . river* (alludes, with sexual innuendo, to catch-
ing trout by tickling their gills); *peculiar* private, off limits

POMPEY   No, but there's a woman with maid by him.
You have not heard of the proclamation, have you?

MISTRESS OVERDONE   What proclamation, man?

94 POMPEY   All houses in the suburbs of Vienna must be
plucked down.

MISTRESS OVERDONE   And what shall become of those in
the city?

98 POMPEY   They shall stand for seed. They had gone down
99 too, but that a wise burgher put in for them.

100 MISTRESS OVERDONE   But shall all our houses of resort in
the suburbs be pulled down?

POMPEY   To the ground, mistress.

MISTRESS OVERDONE   Why, here's a change indeed in the
commonwealth! What shall become of me?

POMPEY   Come, fear not you; good counselors lack no
clients. Though you change your place, you need not
107 change your trade. I'll be your tapster still. Courage,
there will be pity taken on you; you that have worn
your eyes almost out in the service, you will be consid-
110 ered.

MISTRESS OVERDONE   What's to do here, Thomas Tapster? Let's withdraw.

POMPEY   Here comes Signor Claudio, led by the provost
to prison; and there's Madam Juliet.   *Exeunt.*
*Enter Provost, Claudio, Juliet, Officers, Lucio, and two
Gentlemen.*

CLAUDIO
Fellow, why dost thou show me thus to th' world?
Bear me to prison, where I am committed.

PROVOST
117 I do it not in evil disposition,

---

94 *houses* brothels; *suburbs* areas outside city jurisdiction where brothels and
playhouses were located   98 *stand for seed* be maintained for future propagation   99 *burgher* prosperous citizen   100 *houses of resort* brothels   107 *tapster* barman   117 *evil disposition* malicious nature

But from Lord Angelo by special charge.

CLAUDIO

Thus can the demigod Authority

Make us pay down for our offense by weight.   120

The words of heaven: on whom it will, it will;   121

On whom it will not, so. Yet still 'tis just.

LUCIO

Why, how now, Claudio? Whence comes this restraint?

CLAUDIO

From too much liberty, my Lucio, liberty.

As surfeit is the father of much fast,   125

So every scope by the immoderate use   126

Turns to restraint. Our natures do pursue,

Like rats that ravin down their proper bane,   128

A thirsty evil, and when we drink we die.   129

LUCIO   If I could speak so wisely under an arrest, I would   130
send for certain of my creditors. And yet, to say the
truth, I had as lief have the foppery of freedom as the   132
morality of imprisonment. What's thy offense, Claudio?

CLAUDIO

What but to speak of would offend again.

LUCIO   What, is't murder?

CLAUDIO   No.

LUCIO   Lechery?

CLAUDIO   Call it so.

PROVOST   Away, sir, you must go.   140

CLAUDIO

One word, good friend. Lucio, a word with you.

---

120 *pay . . . weight* i.e., pay the heavy bill (alluding to the number and
weight of coins)   121 *words of heaven* biblical prohibitions on loose living
121–22 *on whom . . . just* i.e., heaven inscrutably punishes whomever it will,
but is *just* nevertheless   125 *surfeit* overindulgence, gluttony   126 *scope*
freedom, opportunity   128 *ravin . . . bane* gorge the poison specifically
compounded for them   129 *thirsty* i.e., both causing and experienced as
thirst   132 *I had as lief* I'd just as soon; *foppery* frivolity

LUCIO   A hundred, if they'll do you any good. Is lechery
143 so looked after?

CLAUDIO

144 Thus stands it with me: upon a true contract
     I got possession of Julietta's bed.
146 You know the lady; she is fast my wife
147 Save that we do the denunciation lack
148 Of outward order. This we came not to
149 Only for propagation of a dower
150 Remaining in the coffer of her friends,
151 From whom we thought it meet to hide our love
     Till time had made them for us. But it chances
153 The stealth of our most mutual entertainment
154 With character too gross is writ on Juliet.

LUCIO

     With child, perhaps?

CLAUDIO   Unhappily, even so.
     And the new deputy now for the duke –
157 Whether it be the fault and glimpse of newness,
     Or whether that the body public be
     A horse whereon the governor doth ride,
160 Who, newly in the seat, that it may know
     He can command, lets it straight feel the spur;
162 Whether the tyranny be in his place,
163 Or in his eminence that fills it up,
164 I stagger in – but this new governor
165 Awakes me all the enrollèd penalties
     Which have, like unscoured armor, hung by th' wall
167 So long that nineteen zodiacs have gone round

---

143 *looked after* actively investigated   144 *true contract* legally binding
promise to marry   146 *fast* securely   147 *denunciation* declaration   148
outward order public ceremony   149 *propagation* begetting (i.e., her dowry
wasn't yet fully made up)   150 *coffer* treasure chest; *friends* family   151 *meet*
appropriate   153 *entertainment* enjoyment   154 *gross* large, plainly legible
157 *glimpse* blinding shimmer   162 *place* position   163 *eminence* self-
importance   164 *I stagger in* I'm unsure   165 *Awakes me* revives in my case;
enrollèd recorded in the rolls of the law   167 *zodiacs* i.e., years

And none of them been worn; and for a name   168
Now puts the drowsy and neglected act
Freshly on me. 'Tis surely for a name.   *170*

LUCIO   I warrant it is, and thy head stands so tickle on   171
    thy shoulders that a milkmaid, if she be in love, may
    sigh it off. Send after the duke and appeal to him.

CLAUDIO
    I have done so, but he's not to be found.
    I prithee, Lucio, do me this kind service:
    This day my sister should the cloister enter,   176
    And there receive her approbation.   177
    Acquaint her with the danger of my state;
    Implore her, in my voice, that she make friends
    To the strict deputy; bid herself assay him.   180
    I have great hope in that; for in her youth
    There is a prone and speechless dialect,   182
    Such as move men; beside, she hath prosperous art   183
    When she will play with reason and discourse,   184
    And well she can persuade.

LUCIO   I pray she may, as well for the encouragement of
    the like, which else would stand under grievous imposi-   187
    tion, as for the enjoying of thy life, who I would be
    sorry should be thus foolishly lost at a game of ticktack. 189
    I'll to her.   *190*

CLAUDIO
    I thank you, good friend Lucio.

LUCIO
    Within two hours.

CLAUDIO   Come, officer, away.   *Exeunt.*

                              ✳

---

168 *for a name* i.e., to gain a reputation   **171** *tickle* precariously poised
176 *cloister* nunnery   **177** *approbation* admission as a novice   **180** *assay* as-
sail, try   **182** *prone* ready; *dialect* language   **183** *prosperous* that which pros-
pers   **184** *play with* employ   **187** *the like* i.e., transgressions like Claudio's
187–88 *imposition* penalty   **189** *ticktack* (game similar to backgammon,
here with sexual innuendo)

∾ **I.3** *Enter Duke and Friar Thomas.*

DUKE
No, holy father, throw away that thought;
2 Believe not that the dribbling dart of love
3 Can pierce a complete bosom. Why I desire thee
4 To give me secret harbor hath a purpose
More grave and wrinkled than the aims and ends
Of burning youth.

FRIAR   May your grace speak of it?

DUKE
My holy sir, none better knows than you
8 How I have ever loved the life removed
9 And held in idle price to haunt assemblies
10 Where youth and cost witless bravery keeps.
I have delivered to Lord Angelo,
12 A man of stricture and firm abstinence,
My absolute power and place here in Vienna,
And he supposes me traveled to Poland;
15 For so I have strewed it in the common ear,
And so it is received. Now, pious sir,
You will demand of me why I do this?

FRIAR
Gladly, my lord.

DUKE
We have strict statutes and most biting laws,
20 The needful bits and curbs to headstrong weeds,
21 Which for this fourteen years we have let slip,
22 Even like an o'ergrown lion in a cave,
23 That goes not out to prey. Now, as fond fathers,
Having bound up the threat'ning twigs of birch,

I.3 A friar's cell **2** *dribbling . . . love* weak or misdirected arrow of love **3** *complete* lacking nothing, well-fortified **4** *harbor* lodging **8** *removed* retired **9** *assemblies* large social gatherings **10** *witless bravery* foolish ostentation **12** *stricture* strictness **15** *strewed* spread **21** *fourteen* (cf. *nineteen* in I.2.167) **22** *o'ergrown* fat and lazy **23** *fond* doting

Only to stick it in their children's sight
For terror, not to use, in time the rod
Becomes more mocked than feared. So our decrees,
Dead to infliction, to themselves are dead,   28
And liberty plucks justice by the nose,   29
The baby beats the nurse, and quite athwart   30
Goes all decorum.   31
FRIAR   It rested in your grace
To unloose this tied-up justice when you pleased;
And it in you more dreadful would have seemed   33
Than in Lord Angelo.
DUKE   I do fear, too dreadful.
Sith 'twas my fault to give the people scope,
'Twould be my tyranny to strike and gall them   36
For what I bid them do. For we bid this be done   37
When evil deeds have their permissive pass
And not the punishment. Therefore, indeed, my father,
I have on Angelo imposed the office,   40
Who may, in th' ambush of my name, strike home,   41
And yet my nature never in the fight   42
To do it slander. And to behold his sway   43
I will, as 'twere a brother of your order,
Visit both prince and people. Therefore, I prithee,
Supply me with the habit, and instruct me
How I may formally in person bear   47
Like a true friar. More reasons for this action
At our more leisure shall I render you;
Only this one: Lord Angelo is precise,   50
Stands at a guard with envy, scarce confesses   51

---

28 *Dead to infliction* unenforced **29** *liberty* license **30** *athwart* awry **31** *decorum* good behavior; *rested in* remained in **33** *dreadful* to be feared and respected **36** *gall* hurt (from chafing suffered by horses with ill-fitting saddles) **37–39** *we bid . . . punishment* i.e., in effect, we order people to sin when we permit them to sin without punishment **41** *ambush* cover **42–43** *never . . . slander* never exposed to detraction (?) **43** *sway* rule **47** *formally . . . bear* i.e., conduct myself properly in bearing and manner **50** *precise* correct **51** *Stands . . . envy* is on his guard against malicious detraction

That his blood flows, or that his appetite
Is more to bread than stone. Hence shall we see,
54   If power change purpose, what our seemers be.

                                          Exit [with Friar].

                              *

∾ **I.4** *Enter Isabella and Francisca, a Nun.*

ISABELLA
  And have you nuns no farther privileges?
NUN
  Are not these large enough?
ISABELLA
  Yes, truly. I speak not as desiring more,
  But rather wishing a more strict restraint
5   Upon the sisterhood, the votarists of Saint Clare.
    Lucio within.
LUCIO
  Ho! Peace be in this place.
ISABELLA   Who's that which calls?
NUN
  It is a man's voice. Gentle Isabella,
  Turn you the key, and know his business of him.
  You may, I may not; you are yet unsworn.
10   When you have vowed, you must not speak with men
  But in the presence of the prioress;
  Then, if you speak, you must not show your face,
  Or, if you show your face, you must not speak.
  He calls again; I pray you, answer him.   *[Exit.]*
ISABELLA
  Peace and prosperity; who is't that calls?
    [Enter Lucio.]

---

54 *seemers* those who keep up appearances
  I.4 Within the gate of a nunnery   **5** *votarists* those bound by religious
vows; *Saint Clare* (founder of the strict religious order Isabella wishes to join)

LUCIO

   Hail, virgin, if you be, as those cheek roses

   Proclaim you are no less. Can you so stead me   17

   As bring me to the sight of Isabella,

   A novice of this place, and the fair sister

   To her unhappy brother, Claudio?   20

ISABELLA

   Why "her unhappy brother"? Let me ask,

   The rather for I now must make you know

   I am that Isabella, his sister.

LUCIO

   Gentle and fair, your brother kindly greets you.

   Not to be weary with you, he's in prison.   25

ISABELLA

   Woe me, for what?

LUCIO

   For that which, if myself might be his judge,

   He should receive his punishment in thanks.

   He hath got his friend with child.

ISABELLA

   Sir, make me not your story.   30

LUCIO   'Tis true.

   I would not, though 'tis my familiar sin

   With maids to seem the lapwing and to jest,   32

   Tongue far from heart, play with all virgins so.

   I hold you as a thing enskied and sainted,   34

   By your renouncement an immortal spirit,

   And to be talked with in sincerity,

   As with a saint.

ISABELLA

   You do blaspheme the good in mocking me.

LUCIO

   Do not believe it. Fewness and truth, 'tis thus: 39

---

17 *stead me* assist me   20 *unhappy* unfortunate   25 *weary* tedious   30 *your story* the butt of your jokes   32 *lapwing* species of bird known for deception   34 *enskied* raised to the heavens   39 *Fewness and truth* briefly and truly

40 Your brother and his lover have embraced.
As those that feed grow full, as blossoming time
42 That from the seedness the bare fallow brings
43 To teeming foison, even so her plenteous womb
44 Expresseth his full tilth and husbandry.

ISABELLA
Someone with child by him? My cousin Juliet?

LUCIO
Is she your cousin?

ISABELLA
47 Adoptedly, as schoolmaids change their names
48 By vain though apt affection.

LUCIO   She it is.

ISABELLA
O, let him marry her!

LUCIO   This is the point.
50 The duke is very strangely gone from hence;
51 Bore many gentlemen – myself being one –
In hand, and hope of action; but we do learn
53 By those that know the very nerves of state,
54 His givings-out were of an infinite distance
From his true-meant design. Upon his place,
And with full line of his authority,
Governs Lord Angelo, a man whose blood
Is very snow broth; one who never feels
59 The wanton stings and motions of the sense,
60 But doth rebate and blunt his natural edge
With profits of the mind, study and fast.
62 He – to give fear to use and liberty,
Which have for long run by the hideous law,
As mice by lions – hath picked out an act

---

42 *seedness* sowing; *fallow* plowed soil   43 *foison* abundant harvest   44 *tilth
and husbandry* plowing and good cultivation (punning on "husband" and alluding to sexual penetration)   47 *Adoptedly* by adoption   48 *vain . . . apt*
foolish though fitting their condition   51–52 *Bore . . . In hand* deceived
53 *nerves* sinews   54 *givings-out* pronouncements   59 *motions . . . sense* sexual passions   60 *rebate* blunt   62 *use* custom

Under whose heavy sense your brother's life   65
Falls into forfeit. He arrests him on it,
And follows close the rigor of the statute
To make him an example. All hope is gone,
Unless you have the grace by your fair prayer
To soften Angelo. And that's my pith of business   70
'Twixt you and your poor brother.

ISABELLA
Doth he so seek his life?   72

LUCIO   Has censured him
Already and, as I hear, the provost hath   73
A warrant for's execution.

ISABELLA
Alas, what poor ability's in me
To do him good?   76

LUCIO   Assay the power you have.

ISABELLA
My power, alas, I doubt.

LUCIO   Our doubts are traitors
And make us lose the good we oft might win,
By fearing to attempt. Go to Lord Angelo
And let him learn to know, when maidens sue   80
Men give like gods; but when they weep and kneel,
All their petitions are as freely theirs   82
As they themselves would owe them.   83

ISABELLA
I'll see what I can do.

LUCIO   But speedily.

ISABELLA
I will about it straight,
No longer staying but to give the mother   86
Notice of my affair. I humbly thank you;

---

65 *heavy sense* weighty application   70 *pith* essence   72 *seek his life* aim to
execute him; *censured* judged   73 *provost* officer charged with the punishment of offenders   76 *Assay* put to the test   80 *sue* plead   82 *petitions* re-
quests   83 *As . . . them* i.e., as if they had entirely gotten their own way; *owe*
possess   86 *the mother* mother superior

Commend me to my brother; soon at night
89   I'll send him certain word of my success.
LUCIO
90   I take my leave of you.
ISABELLA   Good sir, adieu.   *Exeunt.*

                                *

∾ **II.1** *Enter Angelo, Escalus, and Servants, Justice.*

ANGELO
We must not make a scarecrow of the law,
2   Setting it up to fear the birds of prey,
And let it keep one shape, till custom make it
Their perch and not their terror.
ESCALUS   Ay, but yet
5   Let us be keen and rather cut a little,
6   Than fall and bruise to death. Alas, this gentleman
Whom I would save had a most noble father.
Let but your honor know,
9   Whom I believe to be most strait in virtue,
10   That, in the working of your own affections,
Had time cohered with place or place with wishing,
12   Or that the resolute acting of your blood
Could have attained th' effect of your own purpose,
14   Whether you had not sometime in your life
Erred in this point which now you censure him,
And pulled the law upon you.
ANGELO
'Tis one thing to be tempted, Escalus,
Another thing to fall. I not deny,
19   The jury passing on the prisoner's life
20   May in the sworn twelve have a thief or two

---

89 *my success* i.e., how I fared
  II.1 A courtroom   2 *fear* frighten   5 *keen* sharp   6 *fall* let fall   9 *strait*
strict, upright   10 *affections* passions   12 *resolute . . . blood* i.e., acting with
resolve on the promptings of your desire   14 *had not* would not have   19
passing delivering a verdict

Guiltier than him they try. What's open made to justice,   21
That justice seizes; what knows the laws
That thieves do pass on thieves? 'Tis very pregnant   23
The jewel that we find, we stoop and take't
Because we see it; but what we do not see
We tread upon, and never think of it.
You may not so extenuate his offense
For I have had such faults, but rather tell me,
When I that censure him do so offend,
Let mine own judgment pattern out my death   30
And nothing come in partial. Sir, he must die.   31
    Enter Provost.

ESCALUS
Be it as your wisdom will.
ANGELO   Where is the provost?
PROVOST
Here, if it like your honor.   33
ANGELO   See that Claudio
Be executed by nine tomorrow morning.
Bring him his confessor, let him be prepared,
For that's the utmost of his pilgrimage.   *[Exit Provost.]*   36
ESCALUS
Well, heaven forgive him, and forgive us all.
Some rise by sin, and some by virtue fall;
Some run from breaks of ice, and answer none,   39
And some condemnèd for a fault alone.   40
    Enter Elbow, Froth, Clown [Pompey], Officers.
ELBOW   Come, bring them away. If these be good people
in a commonweal that do nothing but use their abuses   42
in common houses, I know no law. Bring them away.   43

21–23 *What's . . . thieves* i.e., how can the law know when thieves pass judgment on thieves   23 *'Tis . . . pregnant* it makes sense   30 *pattern out* set the
example for   31 *come in partial* interfere to bias the outcome   33 *like* please
36 *utmost . . . pilgrimage* end of his life   39 *breaks of ice* (obscure); *answer
none* do not have to account for their sins   42 *use their abuses* practice their
wrongdoing   43 *common houses* brothels

ANGELO   How now, sir, what's your name? And what's
the matter?

ELBOW   If it please your honor, I am the poor duke's constable, and my name is Elbow. I do lean upon justice,
sir, and do bring in here before your good honor two
notorious benefactors.

50 ANGELO   Benefactors? Well, what benefactors are they?
Are they not malefactors?

ELBOW   If it please your honor, I know not well what
53 they are; but precise villains they are, that I am sure of,
54 and void of all profanation in the world that good
Christians ought to have.

56 ESCALUS   This comes off well; here's a wise officer.

57 ANGELO   Go to. What quality are they of? Elbow is your
name? Why dost thou not speak, Elbow?

59 POMPEY   He cannot, sir; he's out at elbow.

60 ANGELO   What are you, sir?

61 ELBOW   He, sir, a tapster, sir, parcel bawd; one that serves
a bad woman, whose house, sir, was, as they say,
plucked down in the suburbs, and now she professes a
64 hothouse, which I think is a very ill house too.

ESCALUS   How know you that?

ELBOW   My wife, sir, whom I detest before heaven and
your honor –

ESCALUS   How? Thy wife?

ELBOW   Ay, sir, whom I thank heaven is an honest
70 woman –

ESCALUS   Dost thou detest her therefore?

ELBOW   I say, sir, I will detest myself also, as well as she,
73 that this house, if it be not a bawd's house, it is pity of
her life, for it is a naughty house.

---

53 *precise* i.e., "precious," one of Elbow's many malapropisms   54 *profana-*
tion profanity (which Christians ought *not* to have)   56 *comes off well* sounds
good   57 *quality* social status   59 *out at elbow* threadbare (i.e., devoid of
speech)   61 *parcel bawd* partly a bawd   64 *hothouse* bath house   73–74
pity . . . life i.e., it is too bad

ESCALUS   How dost thou know that, constable?

ELBOW   Marry, sir, by my wife, who, if she had been a
woman cardinally given, might have been accused in   77
fornication, adultery, and all uncleanliness there.

ESCALUS   By the woman's means?   79

ELBOW   Ay, sir, by Mistress Overdone's means; but as she   80
spit in his face, so she defied him.

POMPEY   Sir, if it please your honor, this is not so.

ELBOW   Prove it before these varlets here, thou honorable
man, prove it.

ESCALUS   Do you hear how he misplaces?   85

POMPEY   Sir, she came in great with child, and longing –
saving your honor's reverence – for stewed prunes. Sir,   87
we had but two in the house, which at that very distant
time stood, as it were, in a fruit dish, a dish of some
threepence; your honors have seen such dishes; they are   90
not china dishes, but very good dishes –

ESCALUS   Go to, go to; no matter for the dish, sir.

POMPEY   No, indeed, sir, not of a pin, you are therein in
the right: but to the point. As I say, this Mistress Elbow,
being, as I say, with child, and being great-bellied, and
longing, as I said, for prunes, and having but two in the
dish, as I said, Master Froth here, this very man, having
eaten the rest, as I said, and, as I say, paying for them
very honestly, for, as you know, Master Froth, I could
not give you threepence again –   100

FROTH   No, indeed.

POMPEY   Very well! You being then, if you be remem-
bered, cracking the stones of the foresaid prunes –

FROTH   Ay, so I did, indeed.

POMPEY   Why, very well! I telling you then, if you be re-
membered, that such a one and such a one were past

---

77 *cardinally* (he means "carnally")   79 *By . . . means* i.e., at Overdone's in-
stigation   85 *misplaces* transposes words   87 *stewed prunes* (dish associated
with brothels or "stews," with possible obscene reference to testicles)

107 cure of the thing you wot of, unless they kept very good
     diet, as I told you –

FROTH   All this is true.

110 POMPEY   Why, very well then –

ESCALUS   Come, you are a tedious fool; to the purpose.
     What was done to Elbow's wife, that he hath cause to
113 complain of? Come me to what was done to her.

POMPEY   Sir, your honor cannot come to that yet.

ESCALUS   No, sir, nor I mean it not.

POMPEY   Sir, but you shall come to it, by your honor's
     leave. And I beseech you look into Master Froth here,
     sir, a man of fourscore pound a year, whose father died
119 at Hallowmas. Was't not at Hallowmas, Master Froth?

120 FROTH   Allhallond Eve.

POMPEY   Why, very well; I hope here be truths. He, sir,
122 sitting, as I say, in a lower chair, sir – 'twas in the Bunch
     of Grapes, where indeed you have a delight to sit, have
     you not?

FROTH   I have so, because it is an open room and good
     for winter.

POMPEY   Why, very well then; I hope here be truths.

ANGELO
     This will last out a night in Russia
     When nights are longest there. I'll take my leave,
130 And leave you to the hearing of the cause,
     Hoping you'll find good cause to whip them all.

ESCALUS
132 I think no less. Good morrow to your lordship.

                                        Exit [Angelo].
     Now, sir, come on; what was done to Elbow's wife,
     once more?

POMPEY   Once, sir? There was nothing done to her once.

---

107 *thing you wot of* i.e., syphilis (?)   107–8 *good diet* healthy regimen   113
Come me to bring me to   119 *Hallowmas* All Saints' Day (November 1)
120 *Allhallond Eve* the evening before All Saints' Day (Halloween, October
31)   122 *lower chair* easy chair (?)   122–23 *Bunch of Grapes* (a room at the
inn)   130 *cause* case   132 *I . . . less* i.e., very likely

ELBOW   I beseech you, sir, ask him what this man did to
my wife.

POMPEY   I beseech your honor, ask me.

ESCALUS   Well, sir, what did this gentleman to her?

POMPEY   I beseech you, sir, look in this gentleman's face. *140*
Good Master Froth, look upon his honor; 'tis for a
good purpose. Doth your honor mark his face?

ESCALUS   Ay, sir, very well.

POMPEY   Nay, I beseech you, mark it well.

ESCALUS   Well, I do so.

POMPEY   Doth your honor see any harm in his face?

ESCALUS   Why, no.

POMPEY   I'll be supposed upon a book, his face is the 148
worst thing about him. Good, then, if his face be the
worst thing about him, how could Master Froth do 150
the constable's wife any harm? I would know that of
your honor.

ESCALUS   He's in the right. Constable, what say you to it?

ELBOW   First, an it like you, the house is a respected 154
house; next, this is a respected fellow; and his mistress
is a respected woman.

POMPEY   By this hand, sir, his wife is a more respected
person than any of us all.

ELBOW   Varlet, thou liest; thou liest, wicked varlet. The 159
time is yet to come that she was ever respected with 160
man, woman, or child.

POMPEY   Sir, she was respected with him before he married with her.

ESCALUS   Which is the wiser here, justice or iniquity? Is
this true?

ELBOW   O thou caitiff, O thou varlet, O thou wicked 166
Hannibal! I respected with her before I was married to 167
her? If ever I was respected with her, or she with me, let

---

148 *supposed* i.e., deposed   **154** *respected* i.e., suspected   **159** *Varlet*
scoundrel   **166** *caitiff* wretch   **167** *Hannibal* Carthaginian general, enemy
of Rome (here confused with "cannibal")

not your worship think me the poor duke's officer.
170 Prove this, thou wicked Hannibal, or I'll have mine ac-
171 tion of batt'ry on thee.

ESCALUS If he took you a box o' th' ear, you might have
your action of slander, too.

ELBOW Marry, I thank your good worship for it. What
is't your worship's pleasure I shall do with this wicked
caitiff?

ESCALUS Truly, officer, because he hath some offenses in
178 him that thou wouldst discover if thou couldst, let him
continue in his courses till thou know'st what they are.

180 ELBOW Marry, I thank your worship for it. Thou seest,
thou wicked varlet, now, what's come upon thee. Thou
art to continue now, thou varlet, thou art to continue.

ESCALUS Where were you born, friend?

FROTH Here in Vienna, sir.

185 ESCALUS Are you of fourscore pounds a year?

FROTH Yes, an't please you, sir.

ESCALUS So. *[To Pompey]* What trade are you of, sir?

POMPEY A tapster, a poor widow's tapster.

ESCALUS Your mistress' name?

190 POMPEY Mistress Overdone.

ESCALUS Hath she had any more than one husband?

POMPEY Nine, sir; Overdone by the last.

ESCALUS Nine! Come hither to me, Master Froth. Master Froth, I would not have you acquainted with tap-
195 sters; they will draw you, Master Froth, and you will
196 hang them. Get you gone, and let me hear no more of
you.

FROTH I thank your worship. For mine own part, I
never come into any room in a taphouse but I am
200 drawn in.

ESCALUS Well, no more of it, Master Froth; farewell.
[Exit Froth.]

---

171 *batt'ry* assault | 178 *discover* expose 185 *of* worth 195 *draw you* (1)
entice, (2) drain, (3) gut 196 *hang them* cause them to be hanged

Come you hither to me, master tapster. What's your
name, master tapster?

POMPEY   Pompey.

ESCALUS   What else?

POMPEY   Bum, sir.

ESCALUS   Troth, and your bum is the greatest thing
about you, so that, in the beastliest sense, you are Pom- 208
pey the Great. Pompey, you are partly a bawd, Pompey,
howsoever you color it in being a tapster, are you not? 210
Come, tell me true; it shall be the better for you.

POMPEY   Truly, sir, I am a poor fellow that would live.

ESCALUS   How would you live, Pompey? By being a
bawd? What do you think of the trade, Pompey? Is it a
lawful trade?

POMPEY   If the law would allow it, sir.

ESCALUS   But the law will not allow it, Pompey, nor it
shall not be allowed in Vienna.

POMPEY   Does your worship mean to geld and splay all 219
the youth of the city?   220

ESCALUS   No, Pompey.

POMPEY   Truly, sir, in my poor opinion, they will to't
then. If your worship will take order for the drabs and 223
the knaves, you need not to fear the bawds.

ESCALUS   There is pretty orders beginning, I can tell you;
it is but heading and hanging.   226

POMPEY   If you head and hang all that offend that way
but for ten year together, you'll be glad to give out a 228
commission for more heads. If this law hold in Vienna
ten year, I'll rent the fairest house in it after threepence 230
a bay; if you live to see this come to pass, say Pompey 231
told you so.

208–9 *Pompey the Great* a famous Roman general, rival of Julius Caesar
210 *color* disguise **219** *geld and splay* castrate, neuter **223** *drabs* prostitutes
226 *heading* beheading **228–29** *give . . . commission* issue an order **231**
bay part of a house under a gable

233 ESCALUS   Thank you, good Pompey, and, in requital of
       your prophecy, hark you. I advise you, let me not find
       you before me again upon any complaint whatsoever;
       no, not for dwelling where you do. If I do, Pompey, I
237   shall beat you to your tent and prove a shrewd Caesar
       to you. In plain dealing, Pompey, I shall have you
       whipped. So, for this time, Pompey, fare you well.
240 POMPEY   I thank your worship for your good counsel;
       [Aside] but I shall follow it as the flesh and fortune shall
       better determine.
243   Whip me! No, no, let carman whip his jade;
       The valiant heart's not whipped out of his trade.   Exit.
     ESCALUS   Come hither to me, Master Elbow; come
       hither, master constable. How long have you been in
       this place of constable?
     ELBOW   Seven year and a half, sir.
     ESCALUS   I thought, by the readiness in the office, you
250   had continued in it some time. You say, seven years to-
       gether?
     ELBOW   And a half, sir.
     ESCALUS   Alas, it hath been great pains to you; they do
254   you wrong to put you so oft upon't. Are there not men
255   in your ward sufficient to serve it?
     ELBOW   Faith, sir, few of any wit in such matters. As they
257   are chosen, they are glad to choose me for them. I do it
       for some piece of money, and go through with all.
     ESCALUS   Look you bring me in the names of some six or
260   seven, the most sufficient of your parish.
     ELBOW   To your worship's house, sir?
     ESCALUS   To my house. Fare you well.   [Exit Elbow.]
       What's o'clock, think you?
     JUSTICE   Eleven, sir.
     ESCALUS   I pray you home to dinner with me.

---

233 *requital* recompense   237–38 *beat . . . to you* (when his army was
routed by Julius Caesar's in 48 BCE, Pompey retired to his tent)   243 *carman*
carter; *jade* worn-out horse   254 *put . . . upon't* impose it on you so often
255 *ward* city district   257 *for them* in their place   260 *sufficient* substantial

JUSTICE   I humbly thank you.

ESCALUS

   It grieves me for the death of Claudio,
   But there's no remedy.

JUSTICE

   Lord Angelo is severe.

ESCALUS   It is but needful.

   Mercy is not itself, that oft looks so;   270
   Pardon is still the nurse of second woe.
   But yet poor Claudio; there is no remedy.
   Come, sir.   *Exeunt.*

*

❧ **II.2** *Enter Provost, [and a] Servant.*

SERVANT

   He's hearing of a cause; he will come straight.
   I'll tell him of you.

PROVOST   Pray you, do. *[Exit Servant.]* I'll
   know
   His pleasure; may be he will relent. Alas,
   He hath but as offended in a dream.   4
   All sects, all ages smack of this vice – and he   5
   To die for't!
      Enter Angelo.

ANGELO   Now, what's the matter, provost?

PROVOST

   Is it your will Claudio shall die tomorrow?

ANGELO

   Did not I tell thee, yea? Hadst thou not order?
   Why dost thou ask again?

PROVOST   Lest I might be too rash.

   Under your good correction, I have seen   10

II.2 In Angelo's house 4 *He . . . dream* i.e., both Claudio's state of mind
and the facts make this crime unreal (?) 5 *sects* kinds of people 10 *Under*
subject to

When, after execution, judgment hath
12   Repented o'er his doom.
ANGELO   Go to, let that be mine.
      Do you your office, or give up your place,
      And you shall well be spared.
PROVOST   I   crave   your   honor's
          pardon.
15   What shall be done, sir, with the groaning Juliet?
      She's very near her hour.
ANGELO   Dispose of her
      To some more fitter place, and that with speed.
          [Enter Servant.]
SERVANT
      Here is the sister of the man condemned
      Desires access to you.
ANGELO   Hath he a sister?
PROVOST
20   Ay, my good lord, a very virtuous maid,
      And to be shortly of a sisterhood,
      If not already.
ANGELO   Well, let her be admitted. *[Exit Servant.]*
      See you the fornicatress be removed;
      Let her have needful, but not lavish, means;
25   There shall be order for't.
          Enter Lucio and Isabella.
PROVOST   'Save your honor.
ANGELO
      Stay a little while.
          [To Isabella]   You're welcome. What's your will?
ISABELLA
      I am a woeful suitor to your honor,
      Please but your honor hear me.
ANGELO   Well, what's your suit?
ISABELLA
      There is a vice that most I do abhor,

----

12 *doom* sentence   15 *groaning* i.e., in labor   25 *order* a requisition

And most desire should meet the blow of justice,   *30*
For which I would not plead, but that I must,
For which I must not plead, but that I am
At war 'twixt will and will not.
ANGELO   Well, the matter?
ISABELLA
  I have a brother is condemned to die.
  I do beseech you, let it be his fault,   *35*
  And not my brother.
PROVOST   *[Aside]*   Heaven give thee moving graces.
ANGELO
  Condemn the fault, and not the actor of it?
  Why, every fault's condemned ere it be done.
  Mine were the very cipher of a function,   *39*
  To fine the faults whose fine stands in record,   *40*
  And let go by the actor.
ISABELLA   O just, but severe law!
  I had a brother then. Heaven keep your honor.
LUCIO   *[Aside to Isabella]*
  Give't not o'er so. To him again, entreat him,
  Kneel down before him, hang upon his gown.
  You are too cold. If you should need a pin,
  You could not with more tame a tongue desire it.
  To him, I say.
ISABELLA
  Must he needs die?
ANGELO   Maiden, no remedy.
ISABELLA
  Yes, I do think that you might pardon him,
  And neither heaven nor man grieve at the mercy.   *50*
ANGELO
  I will not do't.
ISABELLA   But can you if you would?

---

35 *let . . . fault* let his fault be condemned   **39** *cipher of a function* meaningless official role   **40** *fine . . . record* the faults already condemned by law

ANGELO

52   Look what I will not, that I cannot do.

ISABELLA

       But might you do't, and do the world no wrong,
54   If so your heart were touched with that remorse
       As mine is to him?

ANGELO

       He's sentenced; 'tis too late.

LUCIO   *[Aside to Isabella]*   You are too cold.

ISABELLA

       Too late? Why, no. I that do speak a word
       May call it back again. Well believe this,
59   No ceremony that to great ones 'longs,
60   Not the king's crown, nor the deputed sword,
       The marshal's truncheon, nor the judge's robe,
       Become them with one half so good a grace
       As mercy does.
       If he had been as you, and you as he,
       You would have slipped like him; but he, like you,
       Would not have been so stern.

ANGELO   Pray you, be gone.

ISABELLA

67   I would to heaven I had your potency,
       And you were Isabel; should it then be thus?
69   No, I would tell what 'twere to be a judge,
70   And what a prisoner.

LUCIO   *[Aside to Isabella]*

                                   Ay, touch him; there's the vein.

ANGELO

       Your brother is a forfeit of the law,
       And you but waste your words.

ISABELLA   Alas, alas;

---

52 *Look what* whatever   54 *remorse* pity   59 *'longs* belongs   60 *deputed sword* emblematic sword of power or justice borne by the one *deputed* to wield it   67 *potency* power   69 *tell* proclaim

Why, all the souls that were were forfeit once,   73
And he that might the vantage best have took,   74
Found out the remedy. How would you be,
If he, which is the top of judgment, should   76
But judge you as you are? O think on that,
And mercy then will breathe within your lips,
Like man new made.   79

ANGELO   Be you content, fair maid,
It is the law, not I, condemn your brother.   80
Were he my kinsman, brother, or my son,   81
It should be thus with him. He must die tomorrow.

ISABELLA
Tomorrow? O, that's sudden; spare him, spare him!
He's not prepared for death. Even for our kitchens
We kill the fowl of season; shall we serve heaven   85
With less respect than we do minister
To our gross selves? Good, good my lord, bethink you.
Who is it that hath died for this offense?
There's many have committed it.

LUCIO   [Aside to Isabella]   Ay, well said.

ANGELO
The law hath not been dead, though it hath slept.   90
Those many had not dared to do that evil
If the first that did th' edict infringe
Had answered for his deed. Now 'tis awake,
Takes note of what is done, and like a prophet
Looks in a glass that shows what future evils,   95
Either new, or by remissness new-conceived,   96
And so in progress to be hatched and born,   97
Are now to have no successive degrees,   98
But, ere they live, to end.

ISABELLA   Yet show some pity.

---

73 *forfeit* lost, doomed 74 *vantage* opportunity 76 *which . . . judgment*
who is the supreme judge 79 *new made* saved, reborn 81 *kinsman* relative
85 *of season* in season 95 *glass* mirror 96 *by remissness* through (our) laxity
97 *in progress* in due course 98 *degrees* stages

ANGELO

100   I show it most of all when I show justice,
      For then I pity those I do not know,
102   Which a dismissed offense would after gall,
103   And do him right that, answering one foul wrong,
      Lives not to act another. Be satisfied;
      Your brother dies tomorrow; be content.

ISABELLA

      So you must be the first that gives this sentence,
      And he, that suffers. O, it is excellent
      To have a giant's strength, but it is tyrannous
      To use it like a giant.

LUCIO   *[Aside to Isabella]*
                          That's well said.

ISABELLA

110   Could great men thunder
      As Jove himself does, Jove would never be quiet,
112   For every pelting, petty officer
      Would use his heaven for thunder,
      Nothing but thunder. Merciful heaven,
      Thou rather with thy sharp and sulphurous bolt
116   Splits the unwedgeable and gnarlèd oak
      Than the soft myrtle; but man, proud man,
      Dressed in a little brief authority,
119   Most ignorant of what he's most assured –
120   His glassy essence – like an angry ape
      Plays such fantastic tricks before high heaven
122   As makes the angels weep; who, with our spleens,
123   Would all themselves laugh mortal.

LUCIO   *[Aside to Isabella]*
      O, to him, to him, wench; he will relent.

---

102 *dismissed* unpunished; *gall* hurt   103 *do him right* serve him well   112
pelting paltry   116 *unwedgeable* unsplittable   119 *assured* confident   120
His . . . essence his own fragile being (?)   122 *spleen* (believed to be the organ
of laughter)   123 *laugh mortal* laugh themselves to death (into human mortality)

He's coming, I perceive't.
PROVOST   *[Aside]*   Pray heaven she win him.
ISABELLA
We cannot weigh our brother with ourself.   126
Great men may jest with saints, 'tis wit in them,   127
But in the less foul profanation.
LUCIO   *[Aside to Isabella]*
Thou'rt i' th' right, girl, more o' that.
ISABELLA
That in the captain's but a choleric word,   130
Which in the soldier is flat blasphemy.
LUCIO   *[Aside to Isabella]*
Art avised o' that? More on't.   132
ANGELO
Why do you put these sayings upon me?   133
ISABELLA
Because authority, though it err like others,
Hath yet a kind of medicine in itself
That skins the vice o' th' top. Go to your bosom,   136
Knock there, and ask your heart what it doth know
That's like my brother's fault. If it confess
A natural guiltiness such as is his,
Let it not sound a thought upon your tongue   *140*
Against my brother's life.
ANGELO   *[Aside]*   She speaks, and 'tis
Such sense that my sense breeds with it. Fare you well.   142
ISABELLA
Gentle my lord, turn back.
ANGELO
I will bethink me. Come again tomorrow.
ISABELLA
Hark how I'll bribe you; good my lord, turn back.

---

126 *our brother* i.e., our fellow man   127 *jest with saints* joke about holy persons or subjects; *wit* cleverness   130 *That* that which; *choleric* angry   132 *avised* informed   133 *put* thrust   136 *skins . . . top* covers over the corruption   142 *sense that . . . breeds* i.e., her good sense excites my sensuality

ANGELO
How! Bribe me?

ISABELLA
Ay, with such gifts that heaven shall share with you.

LUCIO   *[Aside to Isabella]*
You had marred all else.

ISABELLA
149   Not with fond sicles of the tested gold,
150   Or stones whose rate are either rich or poor
151   As fancy values them, but with true prayers
         That shall be up at heaven and enter there
153   Ere sunrise; prayers from preservèd souls,
         From fasting maids whose minds are dedicate
         To nothing temporal.

ANGELO   Well, come to me tomorrow.

LUCIO   *[Aside to Isabella]*
Go to, 'tis well; away.

ISABELLA
Heaven keep your honor safe.

ANGELO   *[Aside]*   Amen.
For I am that way going to temptation,
159   Where prayers cross.

ISABELLA   At what hour tomorrow
160   Shall I attend your lordship?

ANGELO   At any time 'fore noon.

ISABELLA
'Save your honor. *[Exeunt Isabella, Lucio, and Provost.]*

ANGELO   From thee, even from thy virtue!
What's this? What's this? Is this her fault or mine?
The tempter or the tempted, who sins most, ha?
Not she, nor doth she tempt; but it is I
That, lying by the violet in the sun,
Do as the carrion does, not as the flower,

---

149 *fond sicles* foolish shekels (Jewish currency)   **150** *rate are* worth is   **151**
fancy capricious imagination   **153** *preservèd* shielded from vice   **159** *cross*
are at cross purposes

Corrupt with virtuous season. Can it be   167
That modesty may more betray our sense   168
Than woman's lightness? Having waste ground enough,   169
Shall we desire to raze the sanctuary   170
And pitch our evils there? O fie, fie, fie!   171
What dost thou, or what are thou, Angelo?
Dost thou desire her foully for those things
That make her good? O, let her brother live!
Thieves for their robbery have authority
When judges steal themselves. What, do I love her,
That I desire to hear her speak again,
And feast upon her eyes? What is't I dream on?
O cunning enemy that, to catch a saint,   179
With saints dost bait thy hook! Most dangerous   *180*
Is that temptation that doth goad us on
To sin in loving virtue. Never could the strumpet   182
With all her double vigor, art and nature,
Once stir my temper, but this virtuous maid   184
Subdues me quite. Ever till now,
When men were fond, I smiled and wondered how. 186
                                                       Exit.

                              *

∾ **II.3** *Enter Duke [disguised as a friar] and Provost.*

DUKE
   Hail to you, provost – so I think you are.
PROVOST
   I am the provost. What's your will, good friar?
DUKE
   Bound by my charity and my blest order,

---

167 *Corrupt . . . season* rot instead of blooming in the time of growth   **168**
betray . . . sense uncover our sensuality   169 *lightness* lewdness   170 *raze the
sanctuary* demolish the holy place of refuge   171 *pitch our evils* erect our foul
structures (?)   179 *enemy* Satan   182 *strumpet* whore   184 *temper* temper-
ate self-possession   186 *fond* infatuated
   II.3 A prison

I come to visit the afflicted spirits
Here in the prison. Do me the common right
To let me see them and to make me know
The nature of their crimes, that I may minister
To them accordingly.
PROVOST
I would do more than that, if more were needful.
      Enter Juliet.
10   Look, here comes one, a gentlewoman of mine,
11   Who, falling in the flaws of her own youth,
12   Hath blistered her report. She is with child,
And he that got it, sentenced, a young man
More fit to do another such offense
Than die for this.
DUKE
When must he die?
PROVOST   As I do think, tomorrow.
      [To Juliet]
I have provided for you; stay a while
And you shall be conducted.
DUKE
Repent you, fair one, of the sin you carry?
JULIET
20   I do, and bear the shame most patiently.
DUKE
21   I'll teach you how you shall arraign your conscience
And try your penitence, if it be sound,
23   Or hollowly put on.
JULIET   I'll gladly learn.
DUKE
Love you the man that wronged you?
JULIET
Yes, as I love the woman that wronged him.

---

11 *flaws* gusts of passion 12 *blistered . . . report* damaged her reputation
21 *arraign* charge, accuse 23 *hollowly* falsely

DUKE
  So then it seems your most offenseful act
  Was mutually committed?
JULIET   Mutually.
DUKE
  Then was your sin of heavier kind than his.
JULIET
  I do confess it, and repent it, father.
DUKE
  'Tis meet so, daughter, but lest you do repent   30
  As that the sin hath brought you to this shame,   31
  Which sorrow is always toward ourselves, not heaven,
  Showing we would not spare heaven as we love it,   33
  But as we stand in fear –
JULIET
  I do repent me as it is an evil,
  And take the shame with joy.   36
DUKE   There rest.
  Your partner, as I hear, must die tomorrow,
  And I am going with instruction to him.   38
  Grace go with you. Benedicite.   *Exit.*   39
JULIET
  Must die tomorrow! O injurious love,   40
  That respites me a life whose very comfort
  Is still a dying horror.
PROVOST   'Tis pity of him.   *Exeunt.*
                         *

∾ **II.4** *Enter Angelo.*

ANGELO
  When I would pray and think, I think and pray

---

30 *meet* fitting 31 *As that* because 33 *spare* i.e., refrain from offending
36 *There rest* don't change your view 38 *instruction* religious counsel 39
Benedicite bless you
  II.4 In Angelo's house

2   To several subjects. Heaven hath my empty words,
3   Whilst my invention, hearing not my tongue,
         Anchors on Isabel. Heaven in my mouth,
         As if I did but only chew his name,
         And in my heart the strong and swelling evil
7   Of my conception. The state, whereon I studied,
         Is like a good thing, being often read,
         Grown seared and tedious; yea, my gravity,
10   Wherein, let no man hear me, I take pride,
11   Could I, with boot, change for an idle plume
12   Which the air beats for vain. O place, O form,
13   How often dost thou with thy case, thy habit,
         Wrench awe from fools, and tie the wiser souls
         To thy false seeming! Blood, thou art blood.
16   Let's write "good Angel" on the devil's horn,
17   'Tis not the devil's crest. How now, who's there?
         Enter Servant.

SERVANT
         One Isabel, a sister, desires access to you.

ANGELO
         Teach her the way. *[Exit Servant.]* O heavens,
20   Why does my blood thus muster to my heart,
21   Making both it unable for itself,
22   And dispossessing all my other parts
         Of necessary fitness?
         So play the foolish throngs with one that swoons,
         Come all to help him, and so stop the air
         By which he should revive; and even so
27   The general, subject to a well-wished king,

---

2 *several* separate   3 *invention* imagination   7 *conception* thought; *state* statecraft   11 *with boot* profitably; *plume* showy feather   12 *for vain* in vain; *place* high position; *form* ceremony   13 *case* outward covering; *habit* robes 16 *Angel* (punning on "Angelo")   17 *crest* badge, emblem   21 *unable for itself* unable to perform its tasks   22–23 *And . . . fitness* i.e., depriving the rest of the body of what it needs   27 *general* populace; *well-wished king* king who has the people's good wishes

Quit their own part, and in obsequious fondness   28
Crowd to his presence, where their untaught love
Must needs appear offense.   30
   Enter Isabella.
                              How now, fair maid!
ISABELLA
I am come to know your pleasure.
ANGELO
That you might know it would much better please me
Than to demand what 'tis. Your brother cannot live.
ISABELLA
Even so. Heaven keep your honor.
ANGELO
Yet may he live a while, and it may be
As long as you or I; yet he must die.
ISABELLA
Under your sentence?
ANGELO   Yea.
ISABELLA
When, I beseech you? That in his reprieve,   38
Longer or shorter, he may be so fitted   39
That his soul sicken not.   40
ANGELO
Ha! Fie, these filthy vices! It were as good
To pardon him that hath from nature stol'n
A man already made, as to remit   43
Their saucy sweetness that do coin heaven's image   44
In stamps that are forbid. 'Tis all as easy
Falsely to take away a life true made,
As to put mettle in restrainèd means   47
To make a false one.

---

28 *part* places; *obsequious fondness* dutiful affection, overdone deference   **38**
in his reprieve in the interval before execution   **39** *fitted* prepared   **43** *remit*
pardon   **44** *saucy sweetness* impudent enjoyment   **44–45** *coin . . . forbid* i.e.,
counterfeit God's image using forbidden dies (here, unmarried women)   **47**
mettle energy (punning on "metal"); *restrainèd means* forbidden methods

ISABELLA

49   'Tis set down so in heaven, but not in earth.

ANGELO

50   Say you so? Then I shall pose you quickly.
       Which had you rather, that the most just law
       Now took your brother's life, or to redeem him

53   Give up your body to such sweet uncleanness
       As she that he hath stained?

ISABELLA   Sir, believe this,
       I had rather give my body than my soul.

ANGELO

56   I talk not of your soul. Our compelled sins

57   Stand more for number than for account.

ISABELLA   How say you?

ANGELO

58   Nay, I'll not warrant that, for I can speak
       Against the thing I say. Answer to this:

60   I, now the voice of the recorded law,
       Pronounce a sentence on your brother's life.
       Might there not be a charity in sin

63   To save this brother's life?

ISABELLA   Please you to do't,
       I'll take it as a peril to my soul;
       It is no sin at all, but charity.

ANGELO

       Pleased you to do't, at peril of your soul,

67   Were equal poise of sin and charity.

ISABELLA

       That I do beg his life, if it be sin,
       Heaven let me bear it. You granting of my suit,

70   If that be sin, I'll make it my morn prayer

---

49 *'Tis . . . earth* i.e., heaven may regard begetting an illegitimate child as equivalent to murder, but the world does not   **50** *pose* put a difficult question to   **53** *sweet uncleanness* pleasurable defilement   **56** *compelled* constrained   **57** *Stand . . . account* i.e., go on the record, but don't count against us   **58** *warrant* stand by   **60** *recorded* written   **63** *Please* if it pleases   **67** *poise* balance

To have it added to the faults of mine
And nothing of your answer.   72

ANGELO   Nay, but hear me.
Your sense pursues not mine. Either you are ignorant,   73
Or seem so, crafty, and that's not good.   74

ISABELLA
Let me be ignorant, and in nothing good
But graciously to know I am no better.   76

ANGELO
Thus wisdom wishes to appear most bright
When it doth tax itself, as these black masks   78
Proclaim an enshield beauty ten times louder   79
Than beauty could, displayed. But mark me.   80
To be receivèd plain, I'll speak more gross: 81
Your brother is to die.

ISABELLA   So.

ANGELO
And his offense is so, as it appears,
Accountant to the law upon that pain.   85

ISABELLA   True.

ANGELO
Admit no other way to save his life –
As I subscribe not that, nor any other –   88
But, in the loss of question, that you, his sister,   89
Finding yourself desired of such a person   90
Whose credit with the judge, or own great place,
Could fetch your brother from the manacles   92
Of the all-binding law, and that there were
No earthly mean to save him, but that either
You must lay down the treasures of your body
To this supposed, or else to let him suffer,   96
What would you do?

---

72 *nothing . . . answer* nothing for which you need answer   73 *ignorant* un-
comprehending   74 *crafty* craftily   76 *graciously* by God's grace   78 *tax* accuse   79 *enshield* hidden   81 *receivèd* understood   85 *Accountant*
accountable; *pain* penalty   88 *subscribe* assent to   89 *in . . . question* i.e., for
the sake of argument   92 *fetch* release   96 *supposed* imagined person

ISABELLA

    As much for my poor brother as myself.

99   That is, were I under the terms of death,

100   Th' impression of keen whips I'd wear as rubies,

    And strip myself to death as to a bed

102   That longing have been sick for, ere I'd yield

    My body up to shame.

ANGELO   Then must your brother die.

ISABELLA

    And 'twere the cheaper way.

    Better it were a brother died at once

    Than that a sister, by redeeming him,

    Should die for ever.

ANGELO

    Were not you then as cruel as the sentence

    That you have slandered so?

ISABELLA

110   Ignomy in ransom and free pardon

111   Are of two houses; lawful mercy

    Is nothing kin to foul redemption.

ANGELO

    You seemed of late to make the law a tyrant,

114   And rather proved the sliding of your brother

115   A merriment than a vice.

ISABELLA

    O pardon me, my lord, it oft falls out

    To have what we would have, we speak not what we
        mean.

    I something do excuse the thing I hate

    For his advantage that I dearly love.

ANGELO

120   We are all frail.

---

99 *terms of death* death sentence **100** *impression* imprint **102** *longing . . . for* i.e., I have been sick with longing for **110** *Ignomy* ignominy **111** *of two houses* i.e., completely different **114** *sliding* moral dereliction **115** *merriment* prank

ISABELLA   Else let my brother die,
  If not a fedary, but only he   121
  Owe and succeed thy weakness.   122
ANGELO
  Nay, women are frail too.
ISABELLA
  Ay, as the glasses where they view themselves,
  Which are as easy broke as they make forms.   125
  Women, help heaven! Men their creation mar   126
  In profiting by them. Nay, call us ten times frail,
  For we are soft as our complexions are,   128
  And credulous to false prints.   129
ANGELO   I think it well,
  And from this testimony of your own sex –   130
  Since I suppose we are made to be no stronger   131
  Than faults may shake our frames – let me be bold.
  I do arrest your words. Be that you are,   133
  That is, a woman; if you be more, you're none.   134
  If you be one, as you are well expressed   135
  By all external warrants, show it now,   136
  By putting on the destined livery.   137
ISABELLA
  I have no tongue but one. Gentle my lord,   138
  Let me entreat you speak the former language.   139
ANGELO
  Plainly conceive, I love you.   140

---

121 *fedary* confederate   122 *Owe . . . weakness* owns and inherits the frailty you speak of (?)   125 *make forms* produce images   126–27 *Men . . . by them* i.e., men ruin their own created excellence in exploiting frail women   128 *complexions* constitutions   129 *credulous* susceptible; *prints* impressions; *I think it well* that's what I think   131 *I suppose* I take it   131–32 *we . . . our frames* i.e., we are not made so strong that we are invulnerable to evil   133 *I do arrest . . . words* i.e., I take you at your word; *that* that which   134 *if you be . . . none* i.e., if you're more than a woman, you aren't a woman   135 *well expressed* convincingly shown to be   136 *external warrants* outward indications   137 *destined livery* i.e., the garb of sexual service, to which all women are destined   138 *I . . . one* i.e., I can't do double-talk   139 *former language* i.e., previous plain language

ISABELLA
My brother did love Juliet,
And you tell me that he shall die for't.

ANGELO
He shall not, Isabel, if you give me love.

ISABELLA
144 I know your virtue hath a license in't,
Which seems a little fouler than it is,
146 To pluck on others.

ANGELO   Believe me, on mine honor,
My words express my purpose.

ISABELLA
148 Ha! Little honor to be much believed,
And most pernicious purpose. Seeming, seeming!
150 I will proclaim thee, Angelo, look for't!
151 Sign me a present pardon for my brother,
Or with an outstretched throat I'll tell the world aloud
What man thou art.

ANGELO   Who will believe thee, Isabel?
My unsoiled name, th' austereness of my life,
155 My vouch against you, and my place i' th' state,
Will so your accusation overweigh
157 That you shall stifle in your own report
And smell of calumny. I have begun,
159 And now I give my sensual race the rein.
160 Fit thy consent to my sharp appetite,
161 Lay by all nicety and prolixious blushes,
162 That banish what they sue for. Redeem thy brother
By yielding up thy body to my will,
Or else he must not only die the death,
But thy unkindness shall his death draw out

---

144 *license* allowed freedom   146 *pluck on others* trap people into self-betrayal   148 *Little . . . believed* i.e., you have little honor to warrant the extensive belief you solicit   150 *proclaim* denounce; *look for't* expect it   151 *present* immediate   155 *vouch* testimony   157 *report* story   159 *race* (1) steed, (2) speedy motion (?)   161 *nicety* delicacy, prissiness; *prolixious* prolonged (delaying)   162 *That . . . for* that reject what they really ask for

To ling'ring sufferance. Answer me tomorrow,   166
Or, by the affection that now guides me most,   167
I'll prove a tyrant to him. As for you,
Say what you can, my false o'erweighs your true.   *Exit.*

ISABELLA
To whom should I complain? Did I tell this,   170
Who would believe me? O perilous mouths,
That bear in them one and the selfsame tongue,
Either of condemnation or approof,   173
Bidding the law make curtsy to their will,   174
Hooking both right and wrong to th' appetite,
To follow as it draws. I'll to my brother.
Though he hath fall'n by prompture of the blood,   177
Yet hath he in him such a mind of honor
That, had he twenty heads to tender down   179
On twenty bloody blocks, he'd yield them up,   180
Before his sister should her body stoop
To such abhorred pollution.   182
Then, Isabel, live chaste, and, brother, die:
More than our brother is our chastity.
I'll tell him yet of Angelo's request,
And fit his mind to death, for his soul's rest.   *Exit.*

*

∾ **III.1** *Enter Duke [as a friar], Claudio, and Provost.*

DUKE
So then you hope of pardon from Lord Angelo?
CLAUDIO
The miserable have no other medicine
But only hope.
I have hope to live, and am prepared to die.

---

166 *ling'ring sufferance* prolonged torment   **167** *affection* feeling   **170** *Did I tell* if I were to tell   **173** *approof* approval   **174** *make curtsy* bow   **177** *prompture* prompting   **179** *tender* pay   **182** *abhorred pollution* loathed defilement
    III.1 The prison

DUKE

    Be absolute for death; either death or life
    Shall thereby be the sweeter. Reason thus with life:
    If I do lose thee, I do lose a thing
    That none but fools would keep. A breath thou art,
9   Servile to all the skyey influences
10   That dost this habitation where thou keep'st
11   Hourly afflict. Merely, thou art death's fool,
    For him thou labor'st by thy flight to shun,
    And yet run'st toward him still. Thou art not noble,
14   For all th' accommodations that thou bear'st
15   Are nursed by baseness. Thou'rt by no means valiant,
16   For thou dost fear the soft and tender fork
17   Of a poor worm. Thy best of rest is sleep,
18   And that thou oft provok'st, yet grossly fear'st
19   Thy death, which is no more. Thou art not thyself,
20   For thou exists on many a thousand grains
    That issue out of dust. Happy thou art not,
    For what thou hast not, still thou striv'st to get,
23   And what thou hast, forget'st. Thou art not certain,
24   For thy complexion shifts to strange effects,
    After the moon. If thou art rich, thou'rt poor,
26   For, like an ass whose back with ingots bows,
    Thou bear'st thy heavy riches but a journey,
    And death unloads thee. Friend hast thou none,
29   For thine own bowels, which do call thee sire,
30   The mere effusion of thy proper loins,
31   Do curse the gout, serpigo, and the rheum

---

9 *Servile . . . influences* i.e., subject to all the influences of the stars and planets 10 *keep'st* live 11 *Merely, thou art* you are no more than 14 *accommodations* creature comforts 15 *nursed by baseness* have base origins 16 *fork* forked tongue 17 *worm* snake; *thy best . . . is sleep* i.e., you are most tranquil when sleeping 18 *provok'st* call upon 19 *not thyself* i.e., not the whole man you think you are 20 *exists* subsist on; *grains* particles 23 *certain* constant 24–25 *thy complexion . . . moon* your disposition changes capriciously, as the moon changes 26 *ingots* bars of precious metal 29 *bowels* offspring 30 *The mere effusion* no more than the outpouring; *proper* own 31 *serpigo* skin eruption; *rheum* fluid discharge

For ending thee no sooner. Thou hast nor youth nor age,
But as it were an after-dinner's sleep,
Dreaming on both, for all thy blessèd youth
Becomes as agèd, and doth beg the alms   35
Of palsied eld; and when thou art old and rich,   36
Thou hast neither heat, affection, limb, nor beauty,   37
To make thy riches pleasant. What's yet in this
That bears the name of life? Yet in this life   39
Lie hid more thousand deaths; yet death we fear,   40
That makes these odds all even.
CLAUDIO   I humbly thank you.
To sue to live, I find I seek to die,   42
And, seeking death, find life. Let it come on.
     Enter Isabella.
ISABELLA
What, ho! Peace here, grace and good company.
PROVOST
Who's there? Come in, the wish deserves a welcome.
DUKE
Dear sir, ere long I'll visit you again.
CLAUDIO
Most holy sir, I thank you.
ISABELLA
My business is a word or two with Claudio.
PROVOST
And very welcome. Look, signor, here's your sister.
DUKE
Provost, a word with you.   50
PROVOST
As many as you please.
DUKE
Bring me to hear them speak, where I may be concealed.
     [Duke and Provost withdraw.]

---

35 *Becomes as agèd* is as dependent as old age (?)   36 *palsied eld* paralytic old
age 37 *heat* (sexual) energy; *affection* passion; *limb* bodily vitality 39
bears . . . life merits the name of life \ 42 *To sue* i.e., in suing

CLAUDIO
    Now, sister, what's the comfort?
ISABELLA
    Why,
    As all comforts are, most good, most good indeed.
    Lord Angelo, having affairs to heaven,
    Intends you for his swift ambassador,
58 Where you shall be an everlasting leiger.
59 Therefore your best appointment make with speed;
60 Tomorrow you set on.
CLAUDIO   Is there no remedy?
ISABELLA
    None but such remedy as, to save a head,
62 To cleave a heart in twain.
CLAUDIO   But is there any?
ISABELLA
    Yes, brother, you may live.
    There is a devilish mercy in the judge,
    If you'll implore it, that will free your life,
66 But fetter you till death.
CLAUDIO   Perpetual durance?
ISABELLA
    Ay, just – perpetual durance, a restraint,
68 Though all the world's vastidity you had,
69 To a determined scope.
CLAUDIO   But in what nature?
ISABELLA
70 In such a one as, you consenting to't,
71 Would bark your honor from that trunk you bear,
    And leave you naked.
CLAUDIO   Let me know the point.

_____

58 *leiger* resident ambassador   59 *appointment* preparation   60 *set on* depart
62 *cleave . . . in twain* cut in two   66 *fetter* manacle; *durance* imprisonment
68 *Though . . . vastidity* though you had all the world's vastness   69 *determined scope* restricted range; *in what nature* of what kind   71 *bark* strip

ISABELLA

O, I do fear thee, Claudio, and I quake,
Lest thou a feverous life shouldst entertain,   74
And six or seven winters more respect
Than a perpetual honor. Dar'st thou die?
The sense of death is most in apprehension,   77
And the poor beetle that we tread upon
In corporal sufferance finds a pang as great   79
As when a giant dies.   80

CLAUDIO   Why give you me this shame?
Think you I can a resolution fetch
From flow'ry tenderness? If I must die,   82
I will encounter darkness as a bride,
And hug it in mine arms.

ISABELLA

There spake my brother; there my father's grave
Did utter forth a voice. Yes, thou must die;
Thou art too noble to conserve a life
In base appliances. This outward-sainted deputy,   88
Whose settled visage and deliberate word   89
Nips youth i' th' head, and follies doth enew   90
As falcon doth the fowl, is yet a devil;   91
His filth within being cast, he would appear   92
A pond as deep as hell.   93

CLAUDIO   The prenzie Angelo?

ISABELLA

O, 'tis the cunning livery of hell,   94
The damnedest body to invest and cover
In prenzie guards! Dost thou think, Claudio,   96

---

74 *entertain* wish to maintain   77 *sense* painful experience; *apprehension* anticipation   79 *corporal* bodily   80 *shame* mortification   82 *flow'ry* i.e., composed of figures of speech   88 *appliances* remedies; *outward-sainted* saintly seeming   89 *settled visage* unyielding appearance   90 *enew* drive down into the water   91 *fowl* bird   92 *cast* vomited forth   93, 96 *prenzie* (obscure)   94 *livery* servants' or retainers' uniform   96 *guards* trimmings; *Dost . . . think* can you credit

If I would yield him my virginity,
Thou mightst be freed!
CLAUDIO   O heavens, it cannot be.
ISABELLA

99 Yes, he would give't thee, from this rank offense,
100 So to offend him still. This night's the time
    That I should do what I abhor to name,
    Or else thou diest tomorrow.
CLAUDIO   Thou shalt not do't.
ISABELLA
    O, were it but my life,
    I'd throw it down for your deliverance
105 As frankly as a pin.
CLAUDIO   Thanks, dear Isabel.
ISABELLA
    Be ready, Claudio, for your death tomorrow.
CLAUDIO
107 Yes. Has he affections in him,
108 That thus can make him bite the law by th' nose,
109 When he would force it? Sure it is no sin,
110 Or of the deadly seven it is the least.
ISABELLA
    Which is the least?
CLAUDIO
112 If it were damnable, he being so wise,
113 Why would he for the momentary trick
114 Be perdurably fined? O Isabel –
ISABELLA
    What says my brother?
CLAUDIO   Death is a fearful thing.
ISABELLA
    And shamèd life a hateful.

99–100 *he would . . . him still* i.e., from this squalid offense he would give
you means to sin again against his edict **105** *frankly* freely **107** *affections*
desires **108** *bite . . . nose* flout the law **109** *would force* should enforce
112 *were damnable* led to damnation **113** *trick* (1) trifle, (2) sexual act
114 *perdurably fined* punished eternally

CLAUDIO
  Ay, but to die, and go we know not where,
  To lie in cold obstruction and to rot,   118
  This sensible warm motion to become   119
  A kneaded clod; and the delighted spirit   120
  To bathe in fiery floods, or to reside
  In thrilling region of thick-ribbèd ice,   122
  To be imprisoned in the viewless winds   123
  And blown with restless violence round about
  The pendent world; or to be worse than worst   125
  Of those that lawless and incertain thought   126
  Imagine howling, 'tis too horrible.
  The weariest and most loathèd worldly life
  That age, ache, penury, and imprisonment
  Can lay on nature is a paradise   *130*
  To what we fear of death.
ISABELLA
  Alas, alas.
CLAUDIO   Sweet sister, let me live.
  What sin you do to save a brother's life,
  Nature dispenses with the deed so far   134
  That it becomes a virtue.
ISABELLA   O you beast,
  O faithless coward, O dishonest wretch!
  Wilt thou be made a man out of my vice?
  Is't not a kind of incest, to take life
  From thine own sister's shame? What should I think?
  Heaven shield my mother played my father fair,   140
  For such a warpèd slip of wilderness   141
  Ne'er issued from his blood. Take my defiance,
  Die, perish. Might but my bending down

---

118 *obstruction* constriction   **119** *sensible* sentient; *motion* body   **120**
kneaded clod practically shapeless lump of clay; *delighted* capable of delight
122 *thrilling* piercingly cold; *thick-ribbèd* densely packed in ridges   **123**
viewless invisible   **125** *pendent* suspended in space   **126** *incertain* conjec-
tural   **134** *dispenses* pardons   **140** *shield* forbid   **141** *warpèd . . . wilderness*
i.e., wild, deviant shoot (bastard)

Reprieve thee from thy fate, it should proceed.
I'll pray a thousand prayers for thy death,
No word to save thee.

CLAUDIO
Nay, hear me, Isabel.

ISABELLA   O, fie, fie, fie!
148 Thy sin's not accidental, but a trade;
Mercy to thee would prove itself a bawd,
150 'Tis best that thou diest quickly.   *[Going]*

CLAUDIO   O hear me, Isabella.
     [Duke comes forward.]

DUKE
151 Vouchsafe a word, young sister, but one word.

ISABELLA   What is your will?

DUKE   Might you dispense with your leisure, I would by
154 and by have some speech with you. The satisfaction I
would require is likewise your own benefit.

ISABELLA   I have no superfluous leisure; my stay must be
157 stolen out of other affairs, but I will attend you a while.

DUKE   *[Aside to Claudio]* Son, I have overheard what
hath passed between you and your sister. Angelo had
160 never the purpose to corrupt her; only he hath made an
161 assay of her virtue to practice his judgment with the
disposition of natures. She, having the truth of honor
in her, hath made him that gracious denial which he is
most glad to receive. I am confessor to Angelo, and I
know this to be true; therefore prepare yourself to
166 death. Do not satisfy your resolution with hopes that
are fallible; tomorrow you must die. Go to your knees
and make ready.

CLAUDIO   Let me ask my sister pardon. I am so out of
170 love with life that I will sue to be rid of it.

---

148 *accidental* a chance occurrence   151 *Vouchsafe* grant   154 *satisfaction*
result   157 *attend* wait for   161 *assay* trial   161–62 *to practice . . . natures*
test his judgment of character   166 *satisfy* compromise

DUKE   Hold you there. Farewell.   *[Exit Claudio.]*
       [Enter Provost.]
   Provost, a word with you.

PROVOST   What's your will, father?

DUKE   That now you are come, you will be gone. Leave
   me a while with the maid; my mind promises with my   175
   habit no loss shall touch her by my company.

PROVOST   In good time.   *Exit.*

DUKE   The hand that hath made you fair hath made you
   good. The goodness that is cheap in beauty makes   179
   beauty brief in goodness, but grace, being the soul of   180
   your complexion, shall keep the body of it ever fair.
   The assault that Angelo hath made to you, fortune
   hath conveyed to my understanding; and, but that
   frailty hath examples for his falling, I should wonder at 184
   Angelo. How will you do to content this substitute,
   and to save your brother?

ISABELLA   I am now going to resolve him. I had rather   187
   my brother die by the law than my son should be un-
   lawfully born. But O, how much is the good duke deceived in Angelo! If ever he return and I can speak to   190
   him, I will open my lips in vain, or discover his govern- 191
   ment.

DUKE   That shall not be much amiss. Yet, as the matter
   now stands, he will avoid your accusation; he made   194
   trial of you only. Therefore fasten your ear on my advis-
   ings: to the love I have in doing good a remedy presents
   itself. I do make myself believe that you may most up-
   righteously do a poor wronged lady a merited benefit,
   redeem your brother from the angry law, do no stain to
   your own gracious person, and much please the absent   200

175–76 *my mind . . . my habit* my state of mind promises as much as my
habit   179–80 *cheap . . . in goodness* i.e., beauty devoid of goodness will be
short-lived (?)   180 *grace* God-given goodness   180–81 *soul . . . complexion*
essence of your makeup   184 *examples* precedents   187 *resolve* answer   191
discover expose   191–92 *government* conduct   194 *avoid* circumvent

201   duke, if peradventure he shall ever return to have hearing of this business.

ISABELLA   Let me hear you speak farther. I have spirit to
do anything that appears not foul in the truth of my
spirit.

DUKE   Virtue is bold, and goodness never fearful. Have
you not heard speak of Mariana, the sister of Frederick,
208   the great soldier, who miscarried at sea?

ISABELLA   I have heard of the lady, and good words went
210   with her name.

211   DUKE   She should this Angelo have married, was affi-
212   anced by her oath, and the nuptial appointed. Between
213   which time of the contract and limit of the solemnity,
214   her brother Frederick was wracked at sea, having in that
perished vessel the dowry of his sister. But mark how
heavily this befell to the poor gentlewoman. There she
lost a noble and renowned brother, in his love toward
her ever most kind and natural; with him the portion
and sinew of her fortune, her marriage dowry; with
220   both, her combinate husband, this well-seeming Angelo.

ISABELLA   Can this be so? Did Angelo so leave her?

DUKE   Left her in her tears, and dried not one of them
224   with his comfort; swallowed his vows whole, pretend-
225   ing in her discoveries of dishonor; in few, bestowed her
on her own lamentation, which she yet wears for his
227   sake; and he, a marble to her tears, is washed with
them, but relents not.

ISABELLA   What a merit were it in death to take this poor
230   maid from the world! What corruption in this life, that

---

201 *peradventure* perchance   **208** *miscarried* came to grief   **211–12** *affianced* betrothed   **212** *nuptial appointed* marriage arranged   **213** *limit . . .
solemnity* date set for the wedding   **214** *wracked* wrecked   **220** *combinate*
betrothed   **224–25** *pretending . . . dishonor* i.e., alleging evidence of sexual
misconduct on her part   **225–26** *bestowed . . . lamentation* gave her in "marriage" to her own mourning (garb)   **227** *a marble* (1) marble, (2) a monument

it will let this man live! But how out of this can she
avail?   232

DUKE   It is a rupture that you may easily heal; and the
cure of it not only saves your brother, but keeps you
from dishonor in doing it.

ISABELLA   Show me how, good father.

DUKE   This forenamed maid hath yet in her the continuance of her first affection. His unjust unkindness, that
in all reason should have quenched her love, hath, like
an impediment in the current, made it more violent   240
and unruly. Go you to Angelo, answer his requiring   241
with a plausible obedience, agree with his demands to 242
the point. Only refer yourself to this advantage: first, 243
that your stay with him may not be long, that the time
may have all shadow and silence in it, and the place an- 245
swer to convenience. This being granted in course –   246
and now follows all – we shall advise this wronged
maid to stead up your appointment, go in your place. If 248
the encounter acknowledge itself hereafter, it may com- 249
pel him to her recompense; and here, by this is your   250
brother saved, your honor untainted, the poor Mariana
advantaged, and the corrupt deputy scaled. The maid   252
will I frame and make fit for his attempt. If you think 253
well to carry this, as you may, the doubleness of the   254
benefit defends the deceit from reproof. What think
you of it?

ISABELLA   The image of it gives me content already, and I
trust it will grow to a most prosperous perfection.   258

DUKE   It lies much in your holding up. Haste you speed- 259
ily to Angelo. If for this night he entreat you to his bed, 260

---

232 *avail* benefit 241 *requiring* demand 242 *plausible* complaisant
242–43 *to the point* punctiliously 243 *refer . . . advantage* i.e., request him
to meet these conditions 245 *shadow and silence* darkness and secrecy
245–46 *answer . . . convenience* suit your convenience 246 *in course* in due
course 248 *stead up* go instead to 249 *acknowledge itself* becomes public
252 *scaled* weighed in the balance 253 *frame* prepare 254 *carry* conduct
258 *perfection* conclusion 259 *holding up* management

give him promise of satisfaction. I will presently to
262   Saint Luke's; there at the moated grange resides this de-
jected Mariana. At that place call upon me, and dispatch with Angelo, that it may be quickly.

ISABELLA   I thank you for this comfort. Fare you well,
good father.   *Exit.*

*

∾ **III.2** *Enter Elbow, Clown [Pompey], Officers.*

ELBOW   Nay, if there be no remedy for it but that you
will needs buy and sell men and women like beasts, we
3   shall have all the world drink brown and white bastard.

DUKE   O heavens, what stuff is here?

5 POMPEY   'Twas never merry world since, of two usuries,
the merriest was put down, and the worser allowed by
7   order of law a furred gown to keep him warm – and
furred with fox and lamb skins too, to signify that craft,
9   being richer than innocency, stands for the facing.

10 ELBOW   Come your way, sir. Bless you, good father friar.

DUKE   And you, good brother father. What offense hath
this man made you, sir?

ELBOW   Marry, sir, he hath offended the law; and, sir, we
take him to be a thief too, sir, for we have found upon
him, sir, a strange picklock, which we have sent to the
deputy.

DUKE
Fie, sirrah, a bawd, a wicked bawd!
The evil that thou causest to be done,
That is thy means to live. Do thou but think
20 What 'tis to cram a maw or clothe a back
From such a filthy vice; say to thyself,

---

262 *moated grange* country house surrounded by a moat
    III.2 The prison   **3** *bastard* sweet Spanish wine (with obvious pun)   **5**
two usuries i.e., prostitution and moneylending at interest, both "unnatural"
7 *order of law* statute   **9** *stands for the facing* i.e., can afford these trimmings
20 *maw* stomach

From their abominable and beastly touches   22
I drink, I eat, array myself, and live.
Canst thou believe thy living is a life,
So stinkingly depending? Go mend, go mend.   25
POMPEY   Indeed, it does stink in some sort, sir, but yet,
sir, I would prove –
DUKE
Nay, if the devil have given thee proofs for sin,   28
Thou wilt prove his. Take him to prison, officer.   29
Correction and instruction must both work   30
Ere this rude beast will profit.
ELBOW   He must before the deputy, sir; he has given him
warning. The deputy cannot abide a whoremaster; if he
be a whoremonger, and comes before him, he were as   34
good go a mile on his errand.
DUKE
That we were all, as some would seem to be,   36
Free from our faults, as faults from seeming free!
    Enter Lucio.
ELBOW   His neck will come to your waist – a cord, sir.   38
POMPEY   I spy comfort, I cry bail. Here's a gentleman
and a friend of mine.   40
LUCIO   How now, noble Pompey? What, at the wheels of   41
Caesar? Art thou led in triumph? What, is there none
of Pygmalion's images newly made woman to be had   43
now, for putting the hand in the pocket and extracting
it clutched? What reply, ha? What say'st thou to this
tune, matter, and method? Is't not drowned i' th' last   46

---

22 *touches* sexual encounters   25 *depending* dependent   28 *proofs for sin* arguments in favor of sin   29 *prove his* prove yourself his own   30 *Correction*
punishment   34–35 *he were . . . errand* i.e., he is in for some hard going (?)
36–37 *That . . . free* i.e., if only we were all actually as free from fault as some
hypocrites appear to be (?)   38 *His neck . . . your waist* i.e., like your waist,
his neck will have a cord around it   41–42 *the wheels of Caesar* Caesar's chariot (behind which Pompey is being drawn)   43 *Pygmalion's images* i.e., prostitutes (fresh, beautiful women created by art, as in Ovid's *Metamorphoses*,
where Pygmalion's sculpture of Galatea comes to life)   46 *tune* tone; *method*
manner of speaking   46–47 *Is't not . . . rain* (uncertain)

47   rain, ha? What say'st thou, trot? Is the world as it was,
48   man? Which is the way? Is it sad, and few words, or
49   how? The trick of it?

50   DUKE   Still thus, and thus, still worse.

        LUCIO   How doth my dear morsel, thy mistress? Procures
        she still, ha?

53   POMPEY   Troth, sir, she hath eaten up all her beef, and
54   she is herself in the tub.

        LUCIO   Why, 'tis good. It is the right of it; it must be so.
56   Ever your fresh whore and your powdered bawd, an
57   unshunned consequence; it must be so. Art going to
        prison, Pompey?

        POMPEY   Yes, faith, sir.

60   LUCIO   Why, 'tis not amiss, Pompey; farewell. Go, say I
        sent thee thither. For debt, Pompey, or how?

        ELBOW   For being a bawd, for being a bawd.

        LUCIO   Well, then, imprison him. If imprisonment be
64   the due of a bawd, why, 'tis his right. Bawd is he doubt-
65   less, and of antiquity too: bawd-born. Farewell, good
        Pompey; commend me to the prison, Pompey. You will
67   turn good husband now, Pompey, you will keep the
        house.

        POMPEY   I hope, sir, your good worship will be my bail.

70   LUCIO   No, indeed will I not, Pompey, it is not the wear.
        I will pray, Pompey, to increase your bondage; if you
72   take it not patiently, why, your mettle is the more.
        Adieu, trusty Pompey. Bless you, friar.

        DUKE   And you.

75   LUCIO   Does Bridget paint still, Pompey, ha?

---

47 *trot* old crone 48 *sad* unhappy, morose 49 *trick* manner 50 *thus, and thus* i.e., on and on he goes in the same way 53 *eaten . . . beef* (1) used up all her whores (?), (2) run out of sustenance 54 *in the tub* i.e., getting treated for syphilis by exposure to mercury vapor 56 *powdered* (1) pickled in a tub, (2) covered with face powder 57 *unshunned consequence* unavoidable result 64–65 *doubtless* undoubtedly 65 *of antiquity* of old 67–68 *keep the house* stay indoors 70 *not the wear* not in style now 72 *mettle* spirit (punning on "metal") 75 *paint* wear makeup

ELBOW   Come your ways, sir, come.

POMPEY   You will not bail me then, sir?

LUCIO   Then, Pompey, nor now. What news abroad, friar, what news?

ELBOW   Come your ways, sir, come.   80

LUCIO   Go to kennel, Pompey, go.

[Exeunt Elbow, Pompey, and Officers.]

What news, friar, of the duke?

DUKE   I know none. Can you tell me of any?

LUCIO   Some say he is with the emperor of Russia; other   84
some, he is in Rome. But where is he, think you?

DUKE   I know not where, but wheresoever, I wish him well.

LUCIO   It was a mad fantastical trick of him to steal from
the state, and usurp the beggary he was never born to.
Lord Angelo dukes it well in his absence; he puts trans- 90
gression to't.

DUKE   He does well in't.   92

LUCIO   A little more lenity to lechery would do no harm
in him. Something too crabbed that way, friar.   94

DUKE   It is too general a vice, and severity must cure it.

LUCIO   Yes, in good sooth, the vice is of a great kindred, 96
it is well allied; but it is impossible to extirp it quite, 97
friar, till eating and drinking be put down. They say
this Angelo was not made by man and woman after this
downright way of creation. Is it true, think you?   100

DUKE   How should he be made then?

LUCIO   Some report a sea-maid spawned him; some that   102
he was begot between two stockfishes. But it is certain 103
that when he makes water his urine is congealed
ice, that I know to be true. And he is a motion genera- 105
tive, that's infallible.   106

84–85 *other some* others   92 *He ... in't* he does well in doing so   94
crabbed harsh   96 *of a great kindred* (1) well connected, (2) has a large family   97 *extirp* extirpate   100 *downright* down-to-earth   102 *sea-maid* mer-
maid   103 *stockfishes* dried cod   105–6 *motion generative* masculine puppet
106 *infallible* certain

107 DUKE You are pleasant, sir, and speak apace.

LUCIO Why, what a ruthless thing is this in him, for the
109 rebellion of a codpiece to take away the life of a man!
110 Would the duke that is absent have done this? Ere he
111 would have hanged a man for the getting a hundred
bastards, he would have paid for the nursing a thousand. He had some feeling of the sport, he knew the
114 service, and that instructed him to mercy.

115 DUKE I never heard the absent duke much detected for
women. He was not inclined that way.

LUCIO O, sir, you are deceived.

DUKE 'Tis not possible.

119 LUCIO Who? Not the duke? Yes, your beggar of fifty,
120 and his use was to put a ducat in her clackdish. The
121 duke had crotchets in him. He would be drunk, too;
that let me inform you.

DUKE You do him wrong, surely.

124 LUCIO Sir, I was an inward of his. A shy fellow was the
125 duke, and I believe I know the cause of his withdrawing.

DUKE What, I prithee, might be the cause?

LUCIO No, pardon. 'Tis a secret must be locked within
the teeth and the lips. But this I can let you under-
130 stand: the greater file of the subject held the duke to be
wise.

DUKE Wise? Why, no question but he was.

133 LUCIO A very superficial, ignorant, unweighing fellow.

DUKE Either this is envy in you, folly, or mistaking. The
135 very stream of his life and the business he hath helmed

---

107 *pleasant* facetious; *speak apace* run off your mouth 109 *codpiece*
padding or device worn by a man to simulate a large penis (here, meaning
penis) 111 *getting* begetting 114 *service* sexual trade 115 *detected* accused 119 *beggar of fifty* fifty-year-old beggarwoman 120 *clackdish*
wooden begging bowl (with sexual innuendo) 121 *crotchets* strange whims
124 *inward* intimate 125–26 *withdrawing* absenting himself 130 *greater
file* most people 133 *unweighing* unreflecting 135 *stream* regular course;
helmed steered

must, upon a warranted need, give him a better proc- 136
lamation. Let him be but testimonied in his own 137
bringings-forth, and he shall appear to the envious a
scholar, a statesman, and a soldier. Therefore you speak
unskillfully, or, if your knowledge be more, it is much 140
darkened in your malice.

LUCIO   Sir, I know him, and I love him.

DUKE   Love talks with better knowledge, and knowledge
with dearer love.

LUCIO   Come, sir, I know what I know.

DUKE   I can hardly believe that, since you know not
what you speak. But if ever the duke return, as our
prayers are he may, let me desire you to make your an- 148
swer before him. If it be honest you have spoke, you
have courage to maintain it. I am bound to call upon 150
you, and, I pray you, your name?

LUCIO   Sir, my name is Lucio, well known to the duke.

DUKE   He shall know you better, sir, if I may live to report you.

LUCIO   I fear you not.

DUKE   O, you hope the duke will return no more, or you
imagine me too unhurtful an opposite, but indeed I 157
can do you little harm; you'll forswear this again. 158

LUCIO   I'll be hanged first; thou art deceived in me, friar.
But no more of this. Canst thou tell if Claudio die to- 160
morrow or no?

DUKE   Why should he die, sir?

LUCIO   Why? For filling a bottle with a tundish. I would 163
the duke we talk of were returned again. This ungeni- 164
tured agent will unpeople the province with conti-
nency. Sparrows must not build in his house eaves
because they are lecherous. The duke yet would have

---

136 *warranted* authentic 136–37 *proclamation* report 137–38 *testimonied . . . bringings-forth* i.e., let his own accomplishments attest 140 *unskillfully* ignorantly 148–49 *make your answer* justify your allegations 150
call upon summon 157 *opposite* opponent 158 *forswear* deny 163
tundish funnel 164–65 *ungenitured* without genitals

168 dark deeds darkly answered; he would never bring
them to light. Would he were returned. Marry, this
170 Claudio is condemned for untrussing. Farewell, good
friar; I prithee, pray for me. The duke, I say to thee
172 again, would eat mutton on Fridays. He's now past it;
173 yet – and I say to thee – he could mouth with a beggar,
though she smelt brown bread and garlic. Say that I
said so; farewell.   *Exit.*

DUKE
No might nor greatness in mortality
Can censure scape. Back-wounding calumny
The whitest virtue strikes. What king so strong
179 Can tie the gall up in the slanderous tongue?
180 But who comes here?
       Enter Escalus, Provost, and [Officers with] Bawd
       [Mistress Overdone].
ESCALUS   Go, away with her to prison.
MISTRESS OVERDONE   Good my lord, be good to me.
Your honor is accounted a merciful man, good my lord.
184 ESCALUS   Double and treble admonition, and still forfeit
in the same kind! This would make mercy swear, and
play the tyrant.
PROVOST   A bawd of eleven years' continuance, may it
please your honor.
189 MISTRESS OVERDONE   My lord, this is one Lucio's infor-
190 mation against me. Mistress Kate Keepdown was with
child by him in the duke's time; he promised her mar-
192 riage. His child is a year and a quarter old, come Philip
and Jacob. I have kept it myself, and see how he goes
about to abuse me.
ESCALUS   That fellow is a fellow of much license; let him
be called before us. Away with her to prison; go to, no

---

168 *dark deeds . . . answered* secret (sexual) misdeeds dealt with secretly
170 *untrussing* removing his breeches   **172** *mutton* prostitute   **173** *mouth with* kiss   **179** *gall* bitterness   **184** *admonition* warning   **184–85** *still forfeit . . . kind* still culpable for the same offense   **189–90** *information* accusation   **192–93** *Philip and Jacob* the feast of Saints Philip and James (May 1)

more words. *[Exeunt Officers with Mistress Overdone.]*
Provost, my brother Angelo will not be altered; Claudio must die tomorrow. Let him be furnished with di-   199
vines, and have all charitable preparation. If my brother   *200*
wrought by my pity, it should not be so with him.

PROVOST   So please you, this friar hath been with him,
and advised him for th' entertainment of death.   203

ESCALUS   Good even, good father.

DUKE   Bliss and goodness on you!

ESCALUS   Of whence are you?

DUKE
Not of this country, though my chance is now
To use it for my time. I am a brother
Of gracious order, late come from the see,   209
In special business from his holiness.   210

ESCALUS   What news abroad i' th' world?

DUKE   None, but that there is so great a fever on good-   212
ness that the dissolution of it must cure it. Novelty is   213
only in request, and it is as dangerous to be aged in any   214
kind of course as it is virtuous to be constant in any un-
dertaking. There is scarce truth enough alive to make
societies secure, but security enough to make fellow-   217
ships accursed. Much upon this riddle runs the wisdom
of the world. This news is old enough, yet it is every
day's news. I pray you, sir, of what disposition was the   *220*
duke?

ESCALUS   One that, above all other strifes, contended es-   222
pecially to know himself.

DUKE   What pleasure was he given to?

ESCALUS   Rather rejoicing to see another merry, than
merry at anything which professed to make him re-   226

199–200 *furnished with divines* provided with clergy   **203** *entertainment* re-
ception   **209** *see* i.e., Rome, the seat of the papacy   **210** *his holiness* the pope
212–13 *fever on goodness* i.e., goodness is so sick   **213** *dissolution* death
214 *in request* in demand   **214–15** *aged . . . course* steady in any undertak-
ing   **217–18** *security . . . accursed* i.e., enough misplaced trust to make social
relations accursed (?)   **222** *strifes* efforts   **226** *professed* attempted

joice: a gentleman of all temperance. But leave we him
228 to his events, with a prayer they may prove prosperous,
and let me desire to know how you find Claudio pre-
230 pared. I am made to understand that you have lent him
visitation.

232 DUKE He professes to have received no sinister measure
from his judge, but most willingly humbles himself to
234 the determination of justice. Yet had he framed to himself, by the instruction of his frailty, many deceiving
promises of life, which I, by my good leisure, have discredited to him, and now is he resolved to die.

ESCALUS You have paid the heavens your function, and
the prisoner the very debt of your calling. I have la-
240 bored for the poor gentleman to the extremest shore of
my modesty, but my brother justice have I found so severe that he hath forced me to tell him he is indeed justice.

244 DUKE If his own life answer the straitness of his proceed-
ing, it shall become him well; wherein if he chance to
fail, he hath sentenced himself.

ESCALUS I am going to visit the prisoner. Fare you well.
[Exeunt Escalus and Provost.]

DUKE Peace be with you!
He who the sword of heaven will bear
250 Should be as holy as severe;
251 Pattern in himself to know,
252 Grace to stand, and virtue go;
253 More nor less to others paying
Than by self-offenses weighing.
Shame to him whose cruel striking
Kills for faults of his own liking.

---

228 *events* affairs 230–31 *lent . . . visitation* visited him 232 *sinister measure* unjust verdict 234 *framed* conceived 240–41 *extremest shore . . .
modesty* to the limit of propriety 244 *straitness* strictness 251 *Pattern . . .
know* be conscious of himself as a model 252 *Grace . . . go* God's grace to be
steadfast, and virtue to act 253–54 *More . . . weighing* inflicting no more
nor less on others than his own offenses warrant

Twice treble shame on Angelo,
To weed my vice and let his grow.
O, what may man within him hide,
Though angel on the outward side!   260
How may likeness made in crimes,   261
Making practice on the times,   262
To draw with idle spider's strings
Most ponderous and substantial things?   264
Craft against vice I must apply;
With Angelo tonight shall lie
His old betrothèd, but despisèd:
So disguise shall by th' disguisèd
Pay with falsehood, false exacting,   269
And perform an old contracting.   *Exit.*   270

                         *

∾ **IV.1** *Enter Mariana, and Boy singing.*

                    Song.
  Take, O take those lips away,
     That so sweetly were forsworn;
  And those eyes, the break of day,
     Lights that do mislead the morn;   4
  But my kisses bring again, bring again,
  Seals of love, but sealed in vain, sealed in vain.

   Enter Duke [disguised as before].
MARIANA
  Break off thy song, and haste thee quick away.
  Here comes a man of comfort, whose advice
  Hath often stilled my brawling discontent. *[Exit Boy.]*   9
  I cry you mercy, sir, and well could wish   10

----

261 *likeness . . . crimes* (obscure, but suggesting hypocrisy) 262 *practice* deception 264 *ponderous* weighty 269 *exacting* exaction
  IV.1 The moated grange 4 *mislead the morn* falsely promise dawn (?) **9** *brawling* clamorous

You had not found me here so musical.
Let me excuse me, and believe me so,
13   My mirth it much displeased, but pleased my woe.
DUKE
'Tis good, though music oft hath such a charm
To make bad good, and good provoke to harm.
I pray you tell me, hath anybody inquired for me here
today? Much upon this time have I promised here to
meet.
MARIANA   You have not been inquired after. I have sat
20   here all day.
     Enter Isabella.
21   DUKE   I do constantly believe you. The time is come even
now. I shall crave your forbearance a little; may be I will
call upon you anon, for some advantage to yourself.
MARIANA   I am always bound to you.   *Exit.*
DUKE
Very well met, and welcome.
What is the news from this good deputy?
ISABELLA
27   He hath a garden circummured with brick,
Whose western side is with a vineyard backed;
29   And to that vineyard is a planchèd gate,
30   That makes his opening with this bigger key.
31   This other doth command a little door
Which from the vineyard to the garden leads.
There have I made my promise,
Upon the heavy middle of the night,
To call upon him.
DUKE
36   But shall you on your knowledge find this way?

---

13 *My mirth . . . woe* i.e., it conflicted with (my) good spirits but gratified
my sadness 21 *constantly* firmly 27 *circummured* walled about 29
planchèd made of planks 30 *makes his opening* is opened 31 *command*
control 36 *on your knowledge* i.e., from what you have been told

ISABELLA
 I have ta'en a due and wary note upon't.   37
 With whispering and most guilty diligence,
 In action all of precept, he did show me   39
 The way twice o'er.   40
DUKE   Are there no other tokens
 Between you 'greed concerning her observance?   41
ISABELLA
 No, none, but only a repair i' th' dark,   42
 And that I have possessed him my most stay   43
 Can be but brief; for I have made him know
 I have a servant comes with me along,
 That stays upon me, whose persuasion is   46
 I come about my brother.   47
DUKE   'Tis well borne up.
 I have not yet made known to Mariana
 A word of this. What ho, within! Come forth!
  Enter Mariana.
 I pray you, be acquainted with this maid;   *50*
 She comes to do you good.   51
ISABELLA   I do desire the like.
DUKE
 Do you persuade yourself that I respect you?
MARIANA
 Good friar, I know you do, and have found it.
DUKE
 Take then this your companion by the hand,
 Who hath a story ready for your ear.
 I shall attend your leisure, but make haste;   56
 The vaporous night approaches.   57

---

37 *wary* attentive   39 *In action . . . precept* teaching by demonstration   40
tokens signs   41 *observance* prescribed conduct   42 *repair* visit   43 *possessed*
informed   46 *stays upon* waits for; *persuasion* belief   47 *borne up* sustained
51 *the like* the same   56 *attend . . . your leisure* wait until you have finished
and are free again   57 *vaporous* damp

MARIANA
    Will't please you walk aside?
                Exeunt [Mariana and Isabella].

DUKE
    O place and greatness, millions of false eyes
60   Are stuck upon thee. Volumes of report
61   Run with these false, and most contrarious quest
62   Upon thy doings. Thousand escapes of wit
63   Make thee the father of their idle dream,
64   And rack thee in their fancies.
     Enter Mariana and Isabella.
                   Welcome, how agreed?

ISABELLA
    She'll take the enterprise upon her, father,
66   If you advise it.

DUKE   It is not my consent,
    But my entreaty too.

ISABELLA   Little have you to say
    When you depart from him but, soft and low,
69   "Remember now my brother."

MARIANA   Fear me not.

DUKE
70   Nor, gentle daughter, fear you not at all;
71   He is your husband on a precontract;
    To bring you thus together, 'tis no sin,
73   Sith that the justice of your title to him
74   Doth flourish the deceit. Come, let us go;
75   Our corn's to reap, for yet our tithe's to sow.   *Exeunt.*

                        *

---

61 *most contrarious quest* i.e., scrutinize (hunt down) with the utmost perversity and ill will **62** *escapes* sallies **63** *Make ... dream* i.e., make you the source and subject of their frivolous imaginings **64** *rack* distort, misconstrue **66** *not* not only **69** *Fear me not* you can rely on me **70** *fear you not* don't doubt **71** *precontract* legally binding proposal **73** *Sith* since **74** *flourish* embellish **75** *corn's to reap ... sow* i.e., we still have to sow before we can reap the corn; *our tithe* our share (?)

∾ **IV.2** *Enter Provost and Clown [Pompey].*

PROVOST   Come hither, sirrah. Can you cut off a man's   1
head?

POMPEY   If the man be a bachelor, sir, I can; but if he be
a married man, he's his wife's head, and I can never cut   4
off a woman's head.

PROVOST   Come, sir, leave me your snatches, and yield   6
me a direct answer. Tomorrow morning are to die
Claudio and Barnardine. Here is in our prison a common executioner, who in his office lacks a helper. If you
will take it on you to assist him, it shall redeem you   10
from your gyves; if not, you shall have your full time of   11
imprisonment, and your deliverance with an unpitied   12
whipping, for you have been a notorious bawd.

POMPEY   Sir, I have been an unlawful bawd time out of
mind, but yet I will be content to be a lawful hangman.
I would be glad to receive some instruction from my
fellow partner.

PROVOST   What ho, Abhorson! Where's Abhorson there?
Enter Abhorson.

ABHORSON   Do you call, sir?

PROVOST   Sirrah, here's a fellow will help you tomorrow   20
in your execution. If you think it meet, compound   21
with him by the year, and let him abide here with you;
if not, use him for the present and dismiss him. He
cannot plead his estimation with you; he hath been a   24
bawd.

ABHORSON   A bawd, sir? Fie upon him, he will discredit
our mystery.   27

PROVOST   Go to, sir, you weigh equally; a feather will
turn the scale.   *Exit.*

IV.2 The prison   **1** *sirrah* you, sir (mode of address to an inferior)   **4** *his
wife's head* i.e., her superior, according to biblical precept   **6** *snatches* quips
11 *gyves* fetters   **12** *unpitied* merciless   **21** *compound* make an agreement
24 *estimation* good character, reputation   **27** *mystery* craft, calling

30 POMPEY   Pray, sir, by your good favor – for surely, sir, a
31   good favor you have, but that you have a hanging
    look – do you call, sir, your occupation a mystery?

ABHORSON   Ay, sir, a mystery.

34 POMPEY   Painting, sir, I have heard say, is a mystery, and
35   your whores, sir, being members of my occupation,
    using painting, do prove my occupation a mystery. But
    what mystery there should be in hanging, if I should be
    hanged, I cannot imagine.

ABHORSON   Sir, it is a mystery.

40 POMPEY   Proof?

41 ABHORSON   Every true man's apparel fits your thief.

42 POMPEY   If it be too little for your thief, your true man
    thinks it big enough. If it be too big for your thief, your
    thief thinks it little enough; so every true man's apparel
    fits your thief.

    Enter Provost.

PROVOST   Are you agreed?

POMPEY   Sir, I will serve him, for I do find your hangman
    is a more penitent trade than your bawd; he doth of-
49   tener ask forgiveness.

50 PROVOST   You, sirrah, provide your block and your ax to-
    morrow four o'clock.

ABHORSON   Come on, bawd. I will instruct thee in my
    trade; follow.

POMPEY   I do desire to learn, sir; and I hope, if you have
55   occasion to use me for your own turn, you shall find
56   me yare. For truly, sir, for your kindness I owe you a
    good turn.

PROVOST
    Call hither Barnardine and Claudio.

                        Exeunt [Pompey and Abhorson].

---

31 *favor* face   34 *Painting* the art of painting (here implying the application
of cosmetics)   35 *your whores* i.e., whores in general   41 *true* honest
42–43 *If . . . enough* (uncertain)   49 *ask forgiveness* (hangmen asked to be
forgiven by those they were about to execute)   55 *for . . . turn* for your own
execution   56 *yare* ready

Th' one has my pity, not a jot the other,
Being a murderer, though he were my brother.   60
   Enter Claudio.
Look, here's the warrant, Claudio, for thy death.
'Tis now dead midnight, and by eight tomorrow
Thou must be made immortal. Where's Barnardine?

CLAUDIO
As fast locked up in sleep as guiltless labor
When it lies starkly in the traveler's bones.   65
He will not wake.   66

PROVOST   Who can do good on him?
Well, go, prepare yourself.
   [Knocking within.]   But hark, what noise?
Heaven give your spirits comfort.   *[Exit Claudio.]*
                  By and by!
I hope it is some pardon or reprieve
For the most gentle Claudio.   70
   Enter Duke [disguised as before].
                  Welcome, father.

DUKE
The best and wholesom'st spirits of the night
Envelop you, good provost. Who called here of late?

PROVOST
None since the curfew rung.   73

DUKE
Not Isabel?

PROVOST   No.

DUKE   They will then, ere't be long.

PROVOST
What comfort is for Claudio?

DUKE
There's some in hope.

PROVOST   It is a bitter deputy.

---

65 *starkly* stiffly; *traveler* i.e., "travailler," laborer **66** *on* for **73** *curfew* bell
rung at night to signify that laws governing nighttime activities were in force

DUKE
    Not so, not so; his life is paralleled
78   Even with the stroke and line of his great justice.
    He doth with holy abstinence subdue
80   That in himself which he spurs on his power
81   To qualify in others. Were he mealed with that
    Which he corrects, then were he tyrannous,
    But this being so, he's just.
       [Knocking within.]   Now are they come.
                                  [Exit Provost.]

    This is a gentle provost; seldom when
85   The steelèd gaoler is the friend of men.
       [Knocking.]
    How now, what noise? That spirit's possessed with haste
87   That wounds th' unsisting postern with these strokes.
       [Enter Provost.]
PROVOST
    There he must stay until the officer
89   Arise to let him in; he is called up.
DUKE
90   Have you no countermand for Claudio yet,
    But he must die tomorrow?
PROVOST   None, sir, none.
DUKE
    As near the dawning, provost, as it is,
93   You shall hear more ere morning.
PROVOST   Happily
    You something know, yet I believe there comes
95   No countermand; no such example have we.
96   Besides, upon the very siege of justice,
    Lord Angelo hath to the public ear

---

78 *the stroke and line of* i.e., the straight line followed by   81 *qualify* subdue;
mealed stained   85 *steelèd* hardened   87 *unsisting* unresisting (?); *postern*
side door   89 *called up* summoned   93 *Happily* perhaps   95 *example* prece-
dent   96 *siege* seat

Professed the contrary.
　　Enter a Messenger.

DUKE
　This is his lordship's man.

PROVOST
　And here comes Claudio's pardon.　　　　　　　　　*100*

MESSENGER　My lord hath sent you this note, and by me
　this further charge: that you swerve not from the small-
　est article of it, neither in time, matter, or other circum-
　stance. Good morrow, for, as I take it, it is almost day.

PROVOST　I shall obey him.　　　　　*[Exit Messenger.]*

DUKE　*[Aside]*
　This is his pardon, purchased by such sin
　For which the pardoner himself is in.　　　　　*107*
　Hence hath offense his quick celerity,　　　　*108*
　When it is borne in high authority.　　　　　*109*
　When vice makes mercy, mercy's so extended　　*110*
　That for the fault's love is th' offender friended.　*111*
　Now, sir, what news?

PROVOST　I told you. Lord Angelo, belike thinking me
　remiss in mine office, awakens me with this unwonted
　putting on – methinks strangely, for he hath not used it　*115*
　before.

DUKE　Pray you, let's hear.

[PROVOST]　*[Reads] the letter.* "Whatsoever you may hear
　to the contrary, let Claudio be executed by four of the
　clock, and, in the afternoon, Barnardine. For my better　*120*
　satisfaction, let me have Claudio's head sent me by five.
　Let this be duly performed, with a thought that more
　depends on it than we must yet deliver. Thus fail not to　*123*
　do your office, as you will answer it at your peril."
　What say you to this, sir?

---

107 *For . . . in* i.e., of which the pardoner (Angelo) is guilty himself　**108**
quick celerity i.e., speedy vigor　**109** *borne in* propelled by　**111** *friended* be-
friended　**115** *putting on* urging　**123** *must . . . deliver* can yet make known

126 DUKE   What is that Barnardine who is to be executed in th' afternoon?

128 PROVOST   A Bohemian born, but here nursed up and
129 bred; one that is a prisoner nine years old.

130 DUKE   How came it that the absent duke had not either delivered him to his liberty or executed him? I have heard it was ever his manner to do so.

PROVOST   His friends still wrought reprieves for him,
134 and, indeed, his fact, till now in the government of Lord Angelo, came not to an undoubtful proof.

DUKE   It is now apparent?

PROVOST   Most manifest, and not denied by himself.

DUKE   Hath he borne himself penitently in prison? How
139 seems he to be touched?

140 PROVOST   A man that apprehends death no more dreadfully but as a drunken sleep: careless, reckless, and fearless of what's past, present, or to come; insensible of mortality, and desperately mortal.

144 DUKE   He wants advice.

PROVOST   He will hear none. He hath evermore had the
146 liberty of the prison; give him leave to escape hence, he would not. Drunk many times a day, if not many days entirely drunk. We have very oft awaked him, as if to carry him to execution, and showed him a seeming
150 warrant for it; it hath not moved him at all.

151 DUKE   More of him anon. There is written in your brow, provost, honesty and constancy. If I read it not truly,
153 my ancient skill beguiles me; but in the boldness of my
154 cunning I will lay myself in hazard. Claudio, whom
155 here you have warrant to execute, is no greater forfeit to

---

126 *What* who   128 *nursed up* nurtured   129 *prisoner . . . old* i.e., he has been a prisoner for nine years   134 *his fact* deed, crime   139 *touched* affected   140 *apprehends* conceives   144 *wants* lacks   146 *liberty . . . prison* free run of the prison   151 *More . . . anon* more about him in due course   153 *ancient skill* well-tried expertise   153–54 *boldness of my cunning* confidence in my skill   154 *lay . . . hazard* take a gamble   155 *no greater forfeit* no more in jeopardy

the law than Angelo who hath sentenced him. To make
you understand this in a manifested effect, I crave but   157
four days' respite, for the which you are to do me both
a present and a dangerous courtesy.

PROVOST   Pray, sir, in what?   160

DUKE   In the delaying death.

PROVOST   Alack, how may I do it, having the hour lim-   162
ited, and an express command, under penalty, to deliver his head in the view of Angelo? I may make my
case as Claudio's to cross this in the smallest.

DUKE   By the vow of mine order I warrant you. If my instructions may be your guide, let this Barnardine be
this morning executed, and his head borne to Angelo.

PROVOST   Angelo hath seen them both, and will discover   169
the favor.   170

DUKE   O, death's a great disguiser, and you may add to it.
Shave the head, and tie the beard, and say it was the desire of the penitent to be so bared before his death; you
know the course is common. If anything fall to you
upon this more than thanks and good fortune, by the
saint whom I profess, I will plead against it with my
life.

PROVOST   Pardon me, good father, it is against my oath.

DUKE   Were you sworn to the duke or to the deputy?

PROVOST   To him, and to his substitutes.   180

DUKE   You will think you have made no offense, if the
duke avouch the justice of your dealing?   182

PROVOST   But what likelihood is in that?

DUKE   Not a resemblance, but a certainty. Yet since I see
you fearful, that neither my coat, integrity, nor persuasion can with ease attempt you, I will go further than I   186
meant, to pluck all fears out of you. Look you, sir, here

---

157 *in . . . effect* by a revelation   162–63 *limited* stipulated   169–70 *discover the favor* recognize the face   182 *avouch* warrant   186 *attempt* persuade

188   is the hand and seal of the duke; you know the charac-
189   ter, I doubt not, and the signet is not strange to you.
190 PROVOST   I know them both.

DUKE   The contents of this is the return of the duke. You
shall anon overread it at your pleasure, where you shall
find within these two days he will be here. This is a
thing that Angelo knows not, for he this very day re-
ceives letters of strange tenor, perchance of the duke's
death, perchance entering into some monastery, but by
197   chance nothing of what is writ. Look, th' unfolding star
198   calls up the shepherd. Put not yourself into amazement
how these things should be; all difficulties are but easy
200   when they are known. Call your executioner, and off
201   with Barnardine's head; I will give him a present shrift
and advise him for a better place. Yet you are amazed,
but this shall absolutely resolve you. Come away; it is
almost clear dawn.   *Exit [with Provost].*

                              *

~ **IV.3** *Enter Clown [Pompey].*

POMPEY   I am as well acquainted here as I was in our
house of profession. One would think it were Mistress
Overdone's own house, for here be many of her old
customers. First, here's young Master Rash; he's in for a
5   commodity of brown paper and old ginger, ninescore
6   and seventeen pounds, of which he made five marks
ready money. Marry, then ginger was not much in re-
8   quest, for the old women were all dead. Then is there
here one Master Caper, at the suit of Master Three-pile

188–89 *character* handwriting   189 *signet* seal   197 *nothing . . . writ* i.e., the
duke will do otherwise than what is written; *unfolding star* i.e., the morning
star, which tells the shepherd to release the sheep from the fold   198 *amazement* confusion   201 *present shrift* immediate confession and absolution

IV.3 The prison   5 *a commodity* goods bought on credit for resale   6
marks coins valued at two thirds of a pound   8 *old women . . . dead* (old
women were believed to like *ginger*)

the mercer, for some four suits of peach-colored satin, 10
which now peaches him a beggar. Then have we here 11
young Dizzy, and young Master Deep-vow, and Master
Copper-spur, and Master Starve-lackey, the rapier and 13
dagger man, and young Drop-heir that killed lusty
Pudding, and Master Forthright the tilter, and brave 15
Master Shoe-tie the great traveler, and wild Half-can
that stabbed Pots, and I think forty more, all great
doers in our trade, and are now "for the Lord's sake." 18
    Enter Abhorson.

ABHORSON   Sirrah, bring Barnardine hither.
POMPEY   Master Barnardine, you must rise and be 20
hanged, Master Barnardine.
ABHORSON   What ho, Barnardine!
BARNARDINE   *[Within]* A pox o' your throats! Who
makes that noise there? What are you?
POMPEY   Your friends, sir, the hangman. You must be so
good, sir, to rise and be put to death.
BARNARDINE   *[Within]* Away, you rogue, away! I am
sleepy.
ABHORSON   Tell him he must awake, and that quickly
too. 30
POMPEY   Pray, Master Barnardine, awake till you are exe-
cuted, and sleep afterwards.
ABHORSON   Go in to him, and fetch him out.
POMPEY   He is coming, sir, he is coming; I hear his straw
rustle.
    Enter Barnardine.
ABHORSON   Is the ax upon the block, sirrah?
POMPEY   Very ready, sir.
BARNARDINE   How now, Abhorson, what's the news with
you?

---

10 *mercer* dealer in fabrics   **11** *peaches him* i.e., turns him in as   **13–14**
rapier and dagger man fencer (who uses both these weapons)   **15** *tilter*
fighter   **18** *for the Lord's sake* (cry of poor prisoners through the grating, in
begging from passersby)

40 ABHORSON   Truly, sir, I would desire you to clap into
your prayers for, look you, the warrant's come.

BARNARDINE   You rogue, I have been drinking all night;
I am not fitted for't.

POMPEY   O, the better, sir, for he that drinks all night,
45 and is hanged betimes in the morning, may sleep the
sounder all the next day.

Enter Duke [disguised as before].

47 ABHORSON   Look you, sir, here comes your ghostly father. Do we jest now, think you?

DUKE   Sir, induced by my charity, and hearing how
50 hastily you are to depart, I am come to advise you,
comfort you, and pray with you.

BARNARDINE   Friar, not I. I have been drinking hard all
night and I will have more time to prepare me or they
54 shall beat out my brains with billets. I will not consent
to die this day, that's certain.

DUKE   O, sir, you must, and therefore I beseech you look
forward on the journey you shall go.

BARNARDINE   I swear I will not die today for any man's
persuasion.

60 DUKE   But hear you –

BARNARDINE   Not a word. If you have anything to say to
62 me, come to my ward, for thence will not I today. *Exit.*

Enter Provost.

DUKE
63 Unfit to live or die. O gravel heart!
After him, fellows, bring him to the block.

[Exeunt Abhorson and Pompey.]

PROVOST
Now, sir, how do you find the prisoner?

DUKE
66 A creature unprepared, unmeet for death,

---

40 *clap into* begin   45 *betimes* early   47–48 *ghostly father* i.e., spiritual father, confessor   54 *billets* cudgels   62 *ward* prison area   63 *gravel* stony
66 *unmeet* unfitting

And to transport him in the mind he is   67
Were damnable.
PROVOST   Here in the prison, father,
There died this morning of a cruel fever
One Ragozine, a most notorious pirate,   70
A man of Claudio's years, his beard and head
Just of his color. What if we do omit
This reprobate till he were well inclined,   73
And satisfy the deputy with the visage
Of Ragozine, more like to Claudio?
DUKE
O, 'tis an accident that heaven provides.
Dispatch it presently; the hour draws on   77
Prefixed by Angelo. See this be done,   78
And sent according to command, whiles I
Persuade this rude wretch willingly to die.   80
PROVOST
This shall be done, good father, presently.
But Barnardine must die this afternoon,
And how shall we continue Claudio,   83
To save me from the danger that might come
If he were known alive?
DUKE   Let this be done:
Put them in secret holds, both Barnardine and Claudio.   86
Ere twice the sun hath made his journal greeting   87
To yonder generation, you shall find
Your safety manifested.
PROVOST
I am your free dependent.   90
DUKE
Quick, dispatch, and send the head to Angelo.
                                        Exit [Provost].

Now will I write letters to Angelo –

---

67 *transport* dispatch   **73** *reprobate* villain   **77** *presently* at once   **78** *Prefixed*
determined in advance   **83** *continue* keep alive   **86** *holds* cells   **87** *journal*
daily   **90** *your free dependent* freely at your service

The provost, he shall bear them – whose contents
Shall witness to him I am near at home,
95 And that by great injunctions I am bound
To enter publicly. Him I'll desire
97 To meet me at the consecrated fount
A league below the city, and from thence,
99 By cold gradation and well-balanced form,
100 We shall proceed with Angelo.
　　　Enter Provost.

PROVOST
Here is the head. I'll carry it myself.

DUKE
Convenient is it. Make a swift return,
103 For I would commune with you of such things
104 That want no ear but yours.

PROVOST　　　　　　　　　　　I'll make all speed.　　*Exit.*

ISABELLA　*[Within]*
Peace, ho, be here!

DUKE
The tongue of Isabel. She's come to know
If yet her brother's pardon be come hither,
But I will keep her ignorant of her good,
109 To make her heavenly comforts of despair
110 When it is least expected.
　　　Enter Isabella.

ISABELLA　　　　　　　　　　Ho, by your leave!

DUKE
Good morning to you, fair and gracious daughter.

ISABELLA
The better, given me by so holy a man.
Hath yet the deputy sent my brother's pardon?

---

95 *injunctions* (1) commands, (2) compelling necessities　**97** *consecrated fount* holy spring　**99** *cold gradation* unhurried progression; *well-balanced form* orderly process　**103** *commune* talk　**104** *want* require　**109** *To . . . despair* i.e., turn despair into blessed happiness

DUKE
He hath released him, Isabel, from the world.
His head is off and sent to Angelo.

ISABELLA
Nay, but it is not so.

DUKE
It is no other. Show your wisdom, daughter,
In your close patience.   118

ISABELLA
O, I will to him and pluck out his eyes!

DUKE
You shall not be admitted to his sight.   *120*

ISABELLA
Unhappy Claudio, wretched Isabel,
Injurious world, most damnèd Angelo!

DUKE
This nor hurts him nor profits you a jot;
Forbear it therefore, give your cause to heaven.
Mark what I say, which you shall find
By every syllable a faithful verity.
The duke comes home tomorrow – nay, dry your eyes –
One of our covent, and his confessor,   128
Gives me this instance. Already he hath carried   129
Notice to Escalus and Angelo,   *130*
Who do prepare to meet him at the gates,
There to give up their power. If you can, pace your wis-   132
   dom
In that good path that I would wish it go,
And you shall have your bosom on this wretch,   134
Grace of the duke, revenges to your heart,
And general honor.   136

ISABELLA   I am directed by you.

---

118 *close* silent **128** *covent* convent **129** *instance* proof **132** *pace* school
134 *bosom* desire **136** *am* will be

DUKE

This letter then to Friar Peter give;
'Tis that he sent me of the duke's return.
Say, by this token, I desire his company
140   At Mariana's house tonight. Her cause and yours
141   I'll perfect him withal, and he shall bring you
Before the duke; and to the head of Angelo
Accuse him home and home. For my poor self,
144   I am combinèd by a sacred vow
And shall be absent. Wend you with this letter;
Command these fretting waters from your eyes
With a light heart; trust not my holy order
148   If I pervert your course. Who's here?

Enter Lucio.

LUCIO   Good even, friar, where's the provost?
150 DUKE   Not within, sir.

LUCIO   O pretty Isabella, I am pale at mine heart to see
152   thine eyes so red; thou must be patient. I am fain to
153   dine and sup with water and bran; I dare not for my
154   head fill my belly; one fruitful meal would set me to't.
But they say the duke will be here tomorrow. By my
156   troth, Isabel, I loved thy brother. If the old fantastical
157   duke of dark corners had been at home, he had lived.

[Exit Isabella.]

158 DUKE   Sir, the duke is marvelous little beholding to your
reports, but the best is, he lives not in them.

160 LUCIO   Friar, thou knowest not the duke so well as I do.
161   He's a better woodman than thou tak'st him for.

DUKE   Well, you'll answer this one day. Fare ye well.

LUCIO   Nay, tarry, I'll go along with thee; I can tell thee
pretty tales of the duke.

---

141 *perfect* inform fully   144 *combinèd* bound   148 *pervert* deflect, distort
152 *am fain* am constrained   153–54 *for my head* for fear of losing my head
154 *one . . . to't* i.e., a single nourishing meal would be enough to revive my
sexual activity   156 *fantastical* bizarre, whimsical   157 *he had* he would
have   158 *beholding* in your debt   161 *woodman* hunter (here, of women)

DUKE   You have told me too many of him already, sir, if they be true; if not true, none were enough.

LUCIO   I was once before him for getting a wench with child.

DUKE   Did you such a thing?

LUCIO   Yes, marry, did I; but I was fain to forswear it. 170
They would else have married me to the rotten medlar. 171

DUKE   Sir, your company is fairer than honest. Rest you 172
well.

LUCIO   By my troth, I'll go with thee to the lane's end. If bawdy talk offend you, we'll have very little of it. Nay, friar, I am a kind of burr; I shall stick.   *Exeunt.*

*

∾   **IV.4**   *Enter Angelo and Escalus.*

ESCALUS   Every letter he hath writ hath disvouched other. 1

ANGELO   In most uneven and distracted manner. His ac- 2
tions show much like to madness; pray heaven his wisdom be not tainted. And why meet him at the gates 4
and redeliver our authorities there?

ESCALUS   I guess not.

ANGELO   And why should we proclaim it, in an hour before his entering, that if any crave redress of injustice,
they should exhibit their petitions in the street? 9

ESCALUS   He shows his reason for that: to have a dispatch 10
of complaints, and to deliver us from devices hereafter, 11
which shall then have no power to stand against us.

ANGELO
Well, I beseech you let it be proclaimed.

---

170 *fain to forswear* obliged to deny   171 *medlar* fruit that must rot before it
can be enjoyed (metaphorically, women's genitals, here implicitly of a diseased prostitute)   172 *fairer* more appealing
   IV.4 Angelo's house   1 *disvouched* contradicted   2 *uneven* erratic   4
tainted diseased   9 *exhibit* present   10 *dispatch* quick settlement   11 *devices*
stratagems (legal recourses)

14   Betimes i' th' morn I'll call you at your house;
15   Give notice to such men of sort and suit
     As are to meet him.

ESCALUS   I shall, sir. Fare you well.

ANGELO   Good night.   *Exit [Escalus].*

18   This deed unshapes me quite, makes me unpregnant
     And dull to all proceedings. A deflowered maid,
20   And by an eminent body that enforced
     The law against it! But that her tender shame
     Will not proclaim against her maiden loss,
23   How might she tongue me! Yet reason dares her no,
24   For my authority bears off a credent bulk,
     That no particular scandal once can touch
26   But it confounds the breather. He should have lived,
27   Save that his riotous youth with dangerous sense
28   Might in the times to come have ta'en revenge,
     By so receiving a dishonored life
30   With ransom of such shame. Would yet he had lived.
     Alack, when once our grace we have forgot,
32   Nothing goes right; we would, and we would not. *Exit.*

*

∾ **IV.5** *Enter Duke [in his own habit] and Friar Peter.*

DUKE
    These letters at fit time deliver me.
    The provost knows our purpose and our plot.
3   The matter being afoot, keep your instruction,

---

14 *Betimes* early 15 *sort and suit* high rank and retinue 18 *unshapes* undoes; *unpregnant* at a loss 20 *eminent body* highly placed official 23 *tongue* accuse; *reason . . . no* i.e., reason will tell her she dare not 24 *bears . . . bulk* i.e., repels or overbears much that might otherwise be credited 26 *But . . . confounds* without confounding; *breather* i.e., the accuser 27 *sense* inclinations 28–30 *Might . . . shame* (either "might have taken revenge by repeating the crime" or "might have taken revenge on me for the shame of his deliverance") 32 *we . . . not* i.e., we do and don't want to do the things we do
IV.5 Near Vienna 3 *keep your instruction* stick to your orders

And hold you ever to our special drift,   4
Though sometimes you do blench from this to that,   5
As cause doth minister. Go call at Flavius' house,   6
And tell him where I stay; give the like notice
To Valencius, Rowland, and to Crassus,
And bid them bring the trumpets to the gate,   9
But send me Flavius first.   10

FRIAR PETER   It shall be speeded well.
                                            [Exit.]

    Enter Varrius.
DUKE
I thank thee, Varrius; thou hast made good haste.
Come, we will walk; there's other of our friends
Will greet us here anon, my gentle Varrius.   *Exeunt.*

                        *

∾ **IV.6** *Enter Isabella and Mariana.*

ISABELLA
To speak so indirectly I am loath.   1
I would say the truth, but to accuse him so,
That is your part. Yet I am advised to do it,
He says, to veil full purpose.
MARIANA   Be ruled by him.
ISABELLA
Besides, he tells me that if peradventure   5
He speak against me on the adverse side,
I should not think it strange, for 'tis a physic   7
That's bitter to sweet end.
MARIANA
I would Friar Peter –
    Enter [Friar] Peter.

---

4 *drift* aim   5 *blench . . . that* i.e., make tactical adjustments   6 *cause doth minister* necessity dictates   9 *trumpets* trumpeters   10 *speeded well* efficiently performed

    IV.6 A street in Vienna   1 *indirectly* deviously   5 *peradventure* perhaps   7 *physic* medicine

ISABELLA   O, peace, the friar is come.

FRIAR PETER

10 Come, I have found you out a stand most fit,
    Where you may have such vantage on the duke
    He shall not pass you. Twice have the trumpets sounded.

13 The generous and gravest citizens

14 Have hent the gates, and very near upon
    The duke is ent'ring; therefore hence, away.   *Exeunt.*

                            *

 ～ V.1 *Enter Duke, Varrius, Lords, Angelo, Escalus,*
    Lucio, [Provost, Officers, and] Citizens at several
    doors.

DUKE

1   My very worthy cousin, fairly met.
    Our old and faithful friend, we are glad to see you.

ANGELO, ESCALUS

    Happy return be to your royal grace.

DUKE

    Many and hearty thankings to you both.

5   We have made inquiry of you, and we hear
    Such goodness of your justice that our soul
    Cannot but yield you forth to public thanks,

8   Forerunning more requital.

ANGELO   You make my bonds still
    greater.

DUKE

    O, your desert speaks loud, and I should wrong it

10 To lock it in the wards of covert bosom,

11 When it deserves with characters of brass

---

10 *stand* place to stand   13 *generous* wellborn   14 *hent* placed themselves at;
very near upon almost at once
    V.1 The city gates   1 *cousin* (courteous form of address by a ruler to a no-
bleman)   5 *made inquiry . . . you* inquired into your doings   8 *Forerunning . . . requital* preceding further reward   10 *wards . . . bosom* i.e., hidden
recesses of my breast   11 *characters* letters

A forted residence 'gainst the tooth of time   12
And razure of oblivion. Give me your hand,   13
And let the subject see, to make them know
That outward courtesies would fain proclaim   15
Favors that keep within. Come, Escalus,   16
You must walk by us on our other hand,
And good supporters are you.
    Enter [Friar] Peter and Isabella.

FRIAR PETER
Now is your time. Speak loud and kneel before him.

ISABELLA
Justice, O royal duke! Vail your regard   20
Upon a wronged – I would fain have said, a maid.
O worthy prince, dishonor not your eye
By throwing it on any other object
Till you have heard me in my true complaint
And given me justice, justice, justice, justice!

DUKE
Relate your wrongs. In what? By whom? Be brief.
Here is Lord Angelo shall give you justice;
Reveal yourself to him.   28

ISABELLA   O worthy duke,
You bid me seek redemption of the devil.
Hear me yourself, for that which I must speak   30
Must either punish me, not being believed,   31
Or wring redress from you. Hear me, O hear me, here!

ANGELO
My lord, her wits, I fear me, are not firm.
She hath been a suitor to me for her brother,
Cut off by course of justice –

ISABELLA
By course of justice!

---

12 *forted* fortified   13 *razure* erasure   15 *would fain proclaim* i.e., are meant
to signify   16 *Favors . . . within* good intents that remain concealed   20
Vail your regard cast down your look   28 *Reveal* explain   31 *punish me* result
in my punishment

ANGELO

    And she will speak most bitterly and strange.

ISABELLA

    Most strange, but yet most truly, will I speak.

    That Angelo's forsworn, is it not strange?

40   That Angelo's a murderer, is't not strange?

41   That Angelo is an adulterous thief,

    An hypocrite, a virgin-violator,

    Is it not strange, and strange?

DUKE   Nay, it is ten times strange.

ISABELLA

    It is not truer he is Angelo

    Than this is all as true as it is strange.

    Nay, it is ten times true, for truth is truth

    To th' end of reck'ning.

DUKE   Away with her. Poor soul,

48   She speaks this in th' infirmity of sense.

ISABELLA

    O prince, I conjure thee, as thou believ'st

50   There is another comfort than this world,

51   That thou neglect me not with that opinion

    That I am touched with madness. Make not impossible

    That which but seems unlike. 'Tis not impossible

54   But one, the wicked'st caitiff on the ground,

    May seem as shy, as grave, as just, as absolute

    As Angelo. Even so may Angelo,

57   In all his dressings, caracts, titles, forms,

    Be an arch-villain. Believe it, royal prince.

    If he be less, he's nothing; but he's more,

60   Had I more name for badness.

DUKE   By mine honesty,

    If she be mad, as I believe no other,

---

41 *adulterous thief* i.e., thief of women's virginity 48 *infirmity of sense* mental derangement 51 *neglect . . . with* ignore me because of 54 *caitiff* wretch 57 *caracts* insignia of office

Her madness hath the oddest frame of sense, 62
Such a dependency of thing on thing, 63
As e'er I heard in madness.

ISABELLA   O gracious duke,
Harp not on that, nor do not banish reason
For inequality, but let your reason serve 66
To make the truth appear where it seems hid,
And hide the false seems true. 68

DUKE   Many that are not mad
Have sure more lack of reason. What would you say? 69

ISABELLA
I am the sister of one Claudio, 70
Condemned upon the act of fornication
To lose his head, condemned by Angelo.
I, in probation of a sisterhood, 73
Was sent to by my brother, one Lucio
As then the messenger –

LUCIO   That's I, an't like your grace.
I came to her from Claudio, and desired her
To try her gracious fortune with Lord Angelo
For her poor brother's pardon.

ISABELLA   That's he indeed.

DUKE
You were not bid to speak.

LUCIO   No, my good lord,
Nor wished to hold my peace. 80

DUKE   I wish you now, then.
Pray you, take note of it, and when you have
A business for yourself, pray heaven you then
Be perfect. 83

LUCIO   I warrant your honor.

---

62 *frame of sense* rational consistency 63 *dependency* logical connection 66
inequality (1) unequal status, (2) apparent deviation from the established
view (?) 68 *seems* that seems 69 *would you* do you wish to 73 *in probation* a novice 83 *perfect* well prepared

DUKE
  The warrant's for yourself: take heed to't.
ISABELLA
  This gentleman told somewhat of my tale –
LUCIO   Right.
DUKE
  It may be right, but you are i' the wrong
  To speak before your time. Proceed.
ISABELLA   I went
  To this pernicious caitiff deputy –
DUKE
90 That's somewhat madly spoken.
ISABELLA   Pardon it,
91 The phrase is to the matter.
DUKE
  Mended again. The matter: proceed.
ISABELLA
  In brief, to set the needless process by –
  How I persuaded, how I prayed, and kneeled,
95 How he refelled me, and how I replied,
  For this was of much length – the vile conclusion
  I now begin with grief and shame to utter.
  He would not, but by gift of my chaste body
99 To his concupiscible intemperate lust,
100 Release my brother; and after much debatement
101 My sisterly remorse confutes mine honor,
  And I did yield to him; but the next morn betimes,
103 His purpose surfeiting, he sends a warrant
  For my poor brother's head.
DUKE   This is most likely!
ISABELLA
  O, that it were as like as it is true.

---

91 *matter* purpose 95 *refelled* rebuffed 99 *concupiscible* desire-inflamed
101 *remorse* pity 103 *surfeiting* being sexually satiated

DUKE
By heaven, fond wretch, thou know'st not what thou
    speak'st,
Or else thou art suborned against his honor
In hateful practice. First, his integrity   108
Stands without blemish. Next, it imports no reason   109
That with such vehemency he should pursue   110
Faults proper to himself. If he had so offended,   111
He would have weighed thy brother by himself,
And not have cut him off. Someone hath set you on.
Confess the truth, and say by whose advice
Thou cam'st here to complain.
ISABELLA   And is this all?
Then, O you blessèd ministers above,   116
Keep me in patience, and with ripened time
Unfold the evil which is here wrapped up
In countenance. Heaven shield your grace from woe, -   119
As I thus wrongèd hence unbelievèd go.   *120*

DUKE
I know you'd fain be gone. An officer!
To prison with her. Shall we thus permit
A blasting and a scandalous breath to fall   123
On him so near us? This needs must be a practice.   124
Who knew of your intent and coming hither?
ISABELLA
One that I would were here, Friar Lodowick.
DUKE
A ghostly father, belike. Who knows that Lodowick?
LUCIO
My lord, I know him; 'tis a meddling friar,
I do not like the man. Had he been lay, my lord,   129

---

108 *practice* conspiracy   **109** *imports no reason* makes no sense   **110** *pursue*
hunt down   **111** *proper to himself* of his own   **116** *ministers* angels   **119** *In
countenance* under protection of authority and good appearances   **123** *blasting* blighting   **124** *practice* plot   **129** *lay* i.e., a layman

130   For certain words he spake against your grace
131   In your retirement I had swinged him soundly.
DUKE
132   Words against me? This' a good friar, belike,
     And to set on this wretched woman here
     Against our substitute! Let this friar be found.
LUCIO
     But yesternight, my lord, she and that friar,
136   I saw them at the prison; a saucy friar,
137   A very scurvy fellow.
FRIAR PETER
     Blessèd be your royal grace!
     I have stood by, my lord, and I have heard
140   Your royal ear abused. First, hath this woman
     Most wrongfully accused your substitute,
     Who is as free from touch or soil with her
143   As she from one ungot.
DUKE   We did believe no less.
     Know you that Friar Lodowick that she speaks of?
FRIAR PETER
     I know him for a man divine and holy,
146   Not scurvy, nor a temporary meddler,
     As he's reported by this gentleman;
     And, on my trust, a man that never yet
     Did, as he vouches, misreport your grace.
LUCIO
150   My lord, most villainously, believe it.
FRIAR PETER
     Well, he in time may come to clear himself,
     But at this instant he is sick, my lord,
153   Of a strange fever. Upon his mere request,
     Being come to knowledge that there was complaint
     Intended 'gainst Lord Angelo, came I hither,

---

131 *swinged* beaten   **132** *This'* this is   **136** *saucy* impertinent   **137** *scurvy* worthless   **143** *ungot* not yet born   **146** *temporary* temporal   **153** *mere* sole and personal

To speak, as from his mouth, what he doth know
Is true and false, and what he with his oath
And all probation will make up full clear,   158
Whensoever he's convented. First, for this woman,   159
To justify this worthy nobleman,   *160*
So vulgarly and personally accused,
Her shall you hear disprovèd to her eyes,
Till she herself confess it.

DUKE   Good friar, let's hear it.
    [Isabella withdraws, guarded.]
    Enter Mariana.
Do you not smile at this, Lord Angelo?
O heaven, the vanity of wretched fools!
Give us some seats. Come, cousin Angelo,
In this I'll be impartial; be you judge   167
Of your own cause. Is this the witness, friar?
First, let her show her face, and after speak.

MARIANA
Pardon, my lord, I will not show my face   *170*
Until my husband bid me.

DUKE   What, are you married?

MARIANA   No, my lord.

DUKE   Are you a maid?

MARIANA   No, my lord.

DUKE   A widow, then?

MARIANA   Neither, my lord.

DUKE   Why, you are nothing then; neither maid, widow,
nor wife?

LUCIO   My lord, she may be a punk, for many of them   180
are neither maid, widow, nor wife.

DUKE
Silence that fellow. I would he had some cause
To prattle for himself.

LUCIO   Well, my lord.

---

158 *probation* proof   **159** *convented* summoned   **167** *impartial* nonpartici-
pant   **180** *punk* prostitute

MARIANA
    My lord, I do confess I ne'er was married,
    And I confess besides I am no maid.
187   I have known my husband, yet my husband
    Knows not that ever he knew me.
    LUCIO   He was drunk, then, my lord; it can be no better.
190   DUKE   For the benefit of silence, would thou wert so too.
    LUCIO   Well, my lord.
    DUKE
    This is no witness for Lord Angelo.
    MARIANA
    Now I come to't, my lord.
    She that accuses him of fornication,
    In selfsame manner doth accuse my husband,
196   · And charges him, my lord, with such a time
    When, I'll depose, I had him in mine arms,
198   With all th' effect of love.
    ANGELO
    Charges she more than me?
    MARIANA   Not that I know.
    DUKE
200   No? You say your husband?
    MARIANA
    Why, just, my lord, and that is Angelo,
    Who thinks he knows that he ne'er knew my body,
    But knows, he thinks, that he knows Isabel's.
    ANGELO
204   This is a strange abuse. Let's see thy face.
    MARIANA
    My husband bids me; now I will unmask.
        [Unveiling]
    This is that face, thou cruel Angelo,
    Which once thou swor'st was worth the looking on.
208   This is the hand which, with a vowed contract,

---

187 *known* had sex with   196 *with* at   198 *th' effect* the manifestations
204 *abuse* deception   208 *vowed contract* formal betrothal

Was fast belocked in thine. This is the body
That took away the match from Isabel,   *210*
And did supply thee at thy garden house   211
In her imagined person.
DUKE   Know you this woman?
LUCIO
  Carnally, she says.
DUKE   Sirrah, no more!
LUCIO
  Enough, my lord.
ANGELO
  My lord, I must confess I know this woman,
  And five years since there was some speech of marriage
  Betwixt myself and her, which was broke off,
  Partly for that her promisèd proportions   218
  Came short of composition, but in chief   219
  For that her reputation was disvalued   220
  In levity; since which time of five years   221
  I never spake with her, saw her, nor heard from her,
  Upon my faith and honor.
MARIANA   Noble prince,
  As there comes light from heaven and words from
    breath,
  As there is sense in truth and truth in virtue,
  I am affianced this man's wife as strongly   226
  As words could make up vows; and, my good lord,
  But Tuesday night last gone in's garden house
  He knew me as a wife. As this is true,
  Let me in safety raise me from my knees   *230*
  Or else forever be confixèd here   231
  A marble monument.
ANGELO   I did but smile till now.
  Now, good my lord, give me the scope of justice;   233

---

211 *supply* gratify   **218** *proportions* dowry   **219** *composition* what had been agreed upon   **220** *disvalued* discredited   **221** *In levity* for lightness   **226** *affianced* betrothed   **231** *confixèd* fixed in place   **233** *scope* full powers

My patience here is touched. I do perceive
235   These poor informal women are no more
236   But instruments of some more mightier member
      That sets them on. Let me have way, my lord,
      To find this practice out.
DUKE   Ay, with my heart,
      And punish them to your height of pleasure.
240   Thou foolish friar, and thou pernicious woman,
241   Compact with her that's gone, think'st thou thy oaths,
      Though they would swear down each particular saint,
      Were testimonies against his worth and credit
244   That's sealed in approbation? You, Lord Escalus,
      Sit with my cousin; lend him your kind pains
      To find out this abuse, whence 'tis derived.
      There is another friar that set them on;
      Let him be sent for.
FRIAR PETER
      Would he were here, my lord, for he indeed
250   Hath set the women on to this complaint.
      Your provost knows the place where he abides
      And he may fetch him.
DUKE   Go do it instantly.
                                          [Exit Provost.]
253   And you, my noble and well-warranted cousin,
      Whom it concerns to hear this matter forth,
      Do with your injuries as seems you best,
      In any chastisement. I for a while
      Will leave you, but stir not you till you have
258   Well determined upon these slanderers.
ESCALUS
259   My lord, we'll do it throughly.   *Exit [Duke].*

---

235 *informal* disorderly   236 *member* person   241 *Compact with* in league
with   244 *That's sealed in approbation* that carries (my) seal of approval
253 *well-warranted* fully sanctioned and approved   258 *Well determined*
passed well-founded judgment   259 *throughly* thoroughly

Signor Lucio, did not you say you knew that Friar   *260*
Lodowick to be a dishonest person?

LUCIO   *Cucullus non facit monachum;* honest in nothing   *262*
but in his clothes, and one that hath spoke most villainous speeches of the duke.

ESCALUS   We shall entreat you to abide here till he come
and enforce them against him. We shall find this friar a   *266*
notable fellow.

LUCIO   As any in Vienna, on my word.

ESCALUS   Call that same Isabel here once again; I would
speak with her. *[Exit an Attendant.]* Pray you, my lord,   *270*
give me leave to question; you shall see how I'll handle
her.

LUCIO   Not better than he, by her own report.

ESCALUS   Say you?

LUCIO   Marry, sir, I think, if you handled her privately,
she would sooner confess; perchance publicly she'll be
ashamed.

Enter Duke [in his friar's habit], Provost, Isabella
[, and Officers].

ESCALUS   I will go darkly to work with her.   *278*

LUCIO   That's the way, for women are light at midnight.

ESCALUS   Come on, mistress, here's a gentlewoman de-   *280*
nies all that you have said.

LUCIO   My lord, here comes the rascal I spoke of – here
with the provost.

ESCALUS   In very good time. Speak not you to him, till
we call upon you.

LUCIO   Mum.

ESCALUS   Come, sir, did you set these women on to slander Lord Angelo? They have confessed you did.

DUKE   'Tis false.

ESCALUS   How! Know you where you are?   *290*

---

262 *Cucullus . . . monachum* a cowl doesn't make a monk   **266** *enforce* bring
in evidence   **278** *darkly* craftily

DUKE

    Respect to your great place, and let the devil

292   Be sometime honored for his burning throne.

    Where is the duke? 'Tis he should hear me speak.

ESCALUS

    The duke's in us, and we will hear you speak.

295   Look you speak justly.

DUKE

    Boldly at least. But O, poor souls,

    Come you to seek the lamb here of the fox?

    Good night to your redress! Is the duke gone?

    Then is your cause gone too. The duke's unjust,

300   Thus to retort your manifest appeal

    And put your trial in the villain's mouth

    Which here you come to accuse.

LUCIO

    This is the rascal; this is he I spoke of.

ESCALUS

    Why, thou unreverend and unhallowed friar,

    Is't not enough thou hast suborned these women

    To accuse this worthy man but, in foul mouth,

307   And in the witness of his proper ear,

308   To call him villain? And then to glance from him

309   To th' duke himself, to tax him with injustice?

310   Take him hence; to th' rack with him. We'll touse you

    Joint by joint, but we will know his purpose.

    What, unjust?

DUKE   Be not so hot. The duke

    Dare no more stretch this finger of mine than he

    Dare rack his own. His subject am I not,

315   Nor here provincial. My business in this state

    Made me a looker-on here in Vienna,

---

292 *sometime* on occasion   295 *justly* truthfully   300 *retort* turn back; *manifest* plainly true   307 *the witness . . . ear* i.e., in his own hearing   308 *glance* deflect (your accusation)   309 *tax* accuse   310 *touse* tear   315 *provincial* i.e., under the jurisdiction of this province

Where I have seen corruption boil and bubble
Till it o'errun the stew. Laws for all faults,   318
But faults so countenanced that the strong statutes
Stand like the forfeits in a barber's shop,   320
As much in mock as mark.

ESCALUS
Slander to th' state. Away with him to prison.

ANGELO
What can you vouch against him, Signor Lucio?   323
Is this the man that you did tell us of?

LUCIO   'Tis he, my lord. Come hither, goodman bald-   325
pate. Do you know me?

DUKE   I remember you, sir, by the sound of your voice. I
met you at the prison in the absence of the duke.

LUCIO   O, did you so? And do you remember what you
said of the duke?   330

DUKE   Most notedly, sir.   331

LUCIO   Do you so, sir? And was the duke a fleshmonger,   332
a fool, and a coward, as you then reported him to be?

DUKE   You must, sir, change persons with me, ere you
make that my report. You, indeed, spoke so of him, and
much more, much worse.

LUCIO   O thou damnable fellow, did not I pluck thee by
the nose for thy speeches?

DUKE   I protest I love the duke as I love myself.

ANGELO   Hark how the villain would close now, after his   340
treasonable abuses.

ESCALUS   Such a fellow is not to be talked withal; away   342
with him to prison. Where is the provost? Away with
him to prison, lay bolts enough upon him, let him   344
speak no more. Away with those giglets too, and with   345
the other confederate companion.

---

318 *stew* boiling pot (also punning on *stew* as brothel)   **320** *forfeits . . . shop*
i.e., trivial rules of the kind imposed in barbershops   **323** *vouch* give in evidence   **325–26** *baldpate* i.e., monk with a shaven head   **331** *notedly* precisely   **332** *fleshmonger* pimp   **340** *close* i.e., come to a good conclusion
342 *withal* with   **344** *bolts* fetters   **345** *giglets* immoral women

[The Provost lays hands on the Duke.]

DUKE   Stay, sir, stay a while.

ANGELO   What, resists he? Help him, Lucio.

LUCIO   Come, sir, come, sir, come, sir. Foh, sir, why, you
350   bald-pated, lying rascal, you must be hooded, must
you? Show your knave's visage, with a pox to you; show
352   your sheep-biting face, and be hanged an hour. Will't
not off?
         [Pulls off the friar's hood, and discovers the Duke.]

DUKE
    Thou art the first knave that e'er mad'st a duke.
    First, provost, let me bail these gentle three –
         [To Lucio]
    Sneak not away, sir, for the friar and you
    Must have a word anon. Lay hold on him.

LUCIO
    This may prove worse than hanging.

DUKE   *[To Escalus]*
    What you have spoke I pardon. Sit you down,
360   We'll borrow place of him. *[To Angelo]* Sir, by your leave.
361   Hast thou or word or wit or impudence
362   That yet can do thee office? If thou hast,
    Rely upon it till my tale be heard,
364   And hold no longer out.

ANGELO   O my dread lord,
    I should be guiltier than my guiltiness
    To think I can be undiscernible,
    When I perceive your grace, like power divine,
368   Hath looked upon my passes. Then, good prince,
    No longer session hold upon my shame,
370   But let my trial be mine own confession.
371   Immediate sentence, then, and sequent death

---

352 *sheep-biting* villainous (from dogs that bite sheep); *an hour* within the
hour   **361** *or . . . or . . . or* either . . . or . . . or   **362** *do thee office* do you
service   **364** *hold . . . out* admit the truth at once   **368** *passes* deeds   **371** *sequent* consequent

Is all the grace I beg.
DUKE   Come hither, Mariana.
Say, wast thou ere contracted to this woman?
ANGELO
I was, my lord.
DUKE
Go take her hence, and marry her instantly.
Do you the office, friar; which consummate,   376
Return him here again. Go with him, provost.
                    Exeunt [Angelo, with Mariana,
                        Friar Peter, and Provost].

ESCALUS
My lord, I am more amazed at his dishonor
Than at the strangeness of it.
DUKE   Come hither, Isabel.
Your friar is now your prince. As I was then   *380*
Advertising and holy to your business,   *381*
Not changing heart with habit, I am still
Attorneyed at your service.   *383*
ISABELLA   O, give me pardon,
That I, your vassal, have employed and pained   *384*
Your unknown sovereignty.
DUKE   You are pardoned, Isabel;
And now, dear maid, be you as free to us.   *386*
Your brother's death, I know, sits at your heart,
And you may marvel why I obscured myself,
Laboring to save his life, and would not rather
Make rash remonstrance of my hidden power   *390*
Than let him so be lost. O most kind maid,
It was the swift celerity of his death,
Which I did think with slower foot came on,
That brained my purpose; but peace be with him.   *394*
That life is better life past fearing death,

---

376 *consummate* concluded   381 *Advertising* attentive; *holy* honestly devoted   383 *Attorneyed* acting for you   384 *vassal* subject   386 *free* generous
390 *rash remonstrance* blatant demonstration   394 *brained* killed

Than that which lives to fear. Make it your comfort,
So happy is your brother.
  Enter Angelo, Mariana, [Friar] Peter, Provost.

ISABELLA   I do, my lord.

DUKE
For this new-married man approaching here,

399 Whose salt imagination yet hath wronged

400 Your well-defended honor, you must pardon
For Mariana's sake. But as he adjudged your brother,
Being criminal, in double violation
Of sacred chastity, and of promise breach,
Thereon dependent, for your brother's life,
The very mercy of the law cries out

406 Most audible, even from his proper tongue,
"An Angelo for Claudio, death for death!
Haste still pays haste, and leisure answers leisure,
Like doth quit like, and Measure still for Measure."

410 Then, Angelo, thy fault's thus manifested,

411 Which though thou wouldst deny, denies thee vantage.
We do condemn thee to the very block
Where Claudio stooped to death, and with like haste.
Away with him.

MARIANA   O, my most gracious lord,
I hope you will not mock me with a husband.

DUKE
It is your husband mocked you with a husband.
Consenting to the safeguard of your honor,
I thought your marriage fit; else imputation,
For that he knew you, might reproach your life

420 And choke your good to come. For his possessions,
Although by confiscation they are ours,
We do instate and widow you with all,
To buy you a better husband.

MARIANA   O my dear lord,
I crave no other, nor no better man.

———

399 *salt* lecherous **406** *proper* very own **411** *vantage* a way out

DUKE

Never crave him; we are definitive.

MARIANA

Gentle my liege –

DUKE   You do but lose your labor.

Away with him to death. *[To Lucio]* Now, sir, to you.

MARIANA

O my good lord! Sweet Isabel, take my part,
Lend me your knees, and, all my life to come,
I'll lend you all my life to do you service.   430

DUKE

Against all sense you do importune her.   431
Should she kneel down in mercy of this fact,   432
Her brother's ghost his pavèd bed would break,   433
And take her hence in horror.

MARIANA   Isabel,

Sweet Isabel, do yet but kneel by me,
Hold up your hands, say nothing, I'll speak all.
They say best men are molded out of faults,
And, for the most, become much more the better
For being a little bad; so may my husband.
O Isabel, will you not lend a knee?   440

DUKE

He dies for Claudio's death.

ISABELLA   *[Kneeling]*   Most bounteous sir,

Look, if it please you, on this man condemned
As if my brother lived. I partly think
A due sincerity governed his deeds
Till he did look on me. Since it is so,
Let him not die; my brother had but justice,
In that he did the thing for which he died.
For Angelo,
His act did not o'ertake his bad intent,   449
And must be buried but as an intent   450

---

431 *sense* reason   **432** *fact* crime   **433** *pavèd* covered with slabs   **449** *o'er-*
take succeed

451   That perished by the way. Thoughts are no subjects,
     Intents but merely thoughts.

MARIANA   Merely, my lord.

DUKE

453   Your suit's unprofitable; stand up, I say.
     I have bethought me of another fault.
     Provost, how came it Claudio was beheaded
     At an unusual hour?

PROVOST   It was commanded so.

DUKE
     Had you a special warrant for the deed?

PROVOST
     No, my good lord, it was by private message.

DUKE
     For which I do discharge you of your office;

460   Give up your keys.

PROVOST   Pardon me, noble lord;

461   I thought it was a fault, but knew it not,
462   Yet did repent me after more advice;
     For testimony whereof, one in the prison
     That should by private order else have died
     I have reserved alive.

DUKE   What's he?

PROVOST   His name is Barnardine.

DUKE
     I would thou hadst done so by Claudio.
     Go, fetch him hither; let me look upon him.

                                      [Exit Provost.]

ESCALUS
     I am sorry, one so learned and so wise
469   As you, Lord Angelo, have still appeared,
470   Should slip so grossly, both in the heat of blood
     And lack of tempered judgment afterward.

---

451 *Thoughts . . . subjects* i.e., thoughts are not liable to prosecution **453**
unprofitable without merit **461** *knew it not* wasn't certain **462** *more advice*
further reflection **469** *still* always

ANGELO
> I am sorry that such sorrow I procure,   472
> And so deep sticks it in my penitent heart
> That I crave death more willingly than mercy;
> 'Tis my deserving, and I do entreat it.
> > *Enter Barnardine and Provost, Claudio [muffled],*
> > *Juliet.*

DUKE
> Which is that Barnardine?

PROVOST   This, my lord.

DUKE
> There was a friar told me of this man.
> Sirrah, thou art said to have a stubborn soul,
> That apprehends no further than this world,   479
> And squar'st thy life according. Thou'rt condemned,   480
> But, for those earthly faults, I quit them all,   481
> And pray thee take this mercy to provide
> For better times to come. Friar, advise him;
> I leave him to your hand. What muffled fellow's that?

PROVOST
> This is another prisoner that I saved,
> Who should have died when Claudio lost his head,
> As like almost to Claudio as himself.
> > *[Unmuffles Claudio.]*

DUKE *[To Isabella]*
> If he be like your brother, for his sake
> Is he pardoned, and for your lovely sake.
> Give me your hand and say you will be mine;   490
> He is my brother too. But fitter time for that.
> By this Lord Angelo perceives he's safe;
> Methinks I see a quick'ning in his eye.
> Well, Angelo, your evil quits you well.   494
> Look that you love your wife, her worth, worth yours.   495

---

472 *procure* cause   479 *apprehends* envisions   480 *squar'st* regulate   481
quit pardon   494 *quits* requites   495 *worth . . . yours* her worth equals yours

496 I find an apt remission in myself,
497 And yet here's one in place I cannot pardon.
       [To Lucio]
       You, sirrah, that knew me for a fool, a coward,
499 One all of luxury, an ass, a madman,
500 Wherein have I so deserved of you,
       That you extol me thus?

LUCIO 'Faith, my lord, I spoke it but according to the
503 trick. If you will hang me for it, you may, but I had
       rather it would please you, I might be whipped.

DUKE
       Whipped first, sir, and hanged after.
       Proclaim it, provost, round about the city,
       If any woman wronged by this lewd fellow –
       As I have heard him swear himself there's one
       Whom he begot with child – let her appear,
510 And he shall marry her. The nuptial finished,
       Let him be whipped and hanged.

LUCIO I beseech your highness, do not marry me to a
       whore. Your highness said even now, I made you a
       duke; good my lord, do not recompense me in making
       me a cuckold.

DUKE
       Upon mine honor, thou shalt marry her.
       Thy slanders I forgive, and therewithal
518 Remit thy other forfeits. Take him to prison,
       And see our pleasure herein executed.

520 LUCIO Marrying a punk, my lord, is pressing to death,
       whipping, and hanging.

DUKE
       Slandering a prince deserves it.
                                  [Exeunt Officers with Lucio.]

---

496 *apt remission* ready forgiveness **497** *in place* here **499** *luxury* lechery
503 *trick* fashion **518** *Remit . . . forfeits* waive your other penalties **520**
pressing . . . death torture in which victims are pressed under progressively
heavier weights until they are crushed

She, Claudio, that you wronged, look you restore.
Joy to you, Mariana; love her, Angelo;
I have confessed her and I know her virtue.
Thanks, good friend Escalus, for thy much goodness;
There's more behind that is more gratulate.   527
Thanks, provost, for thy care and secrecy;
We shall employ thee in a worthier place.
Forgive him, Angelo, that brought you home   530
The head of Ragozine for Claudio's;
Th' offense pardons itself. Dear Isabel,
I have a motion much imports your good,   533
Whereto if you'll a willing ear incline,
What's mine is yours, and what is yours is mine.
So, bring us to our palace, where we'll show
What's yet behind, that's meet you all should know.   537

                                              [Exeunt.]

---

527 *gratulate* gratifying   533 *motion* proposition   537 *yet behind* yet to
come; *meet* proper